SCAVENGER CHAOS ZONE

Paul Stewart is a highly regarded and award-winning author of books for young readers – everything from picture books to football stories, fantasy, sci-fi and horror. His first book was published in 1988 and he has since had over fifty titles published.

Chris Riddell is an accomplished artist and political cartoonist for the *Observer*. His books have won many awards, including the Kate Greenaway Medal, the Nestlé Children's Book Prize and the Red House Children's Book Award. *Goth Girl and the Ghost of a Mouse* won the Costa Children's Book Award in 2013.

Paul and Chris first met at their sons' nursery school and decided to work together (they can't remember why!). Since then their books have included the Blobheads series, The Edge Chronicles, the Muddle Earth books and the Far-Flung Adventures, which include *Fergus Crane*, Gold Smarties Prize Winner, *Corby Flood* and *Hugo*

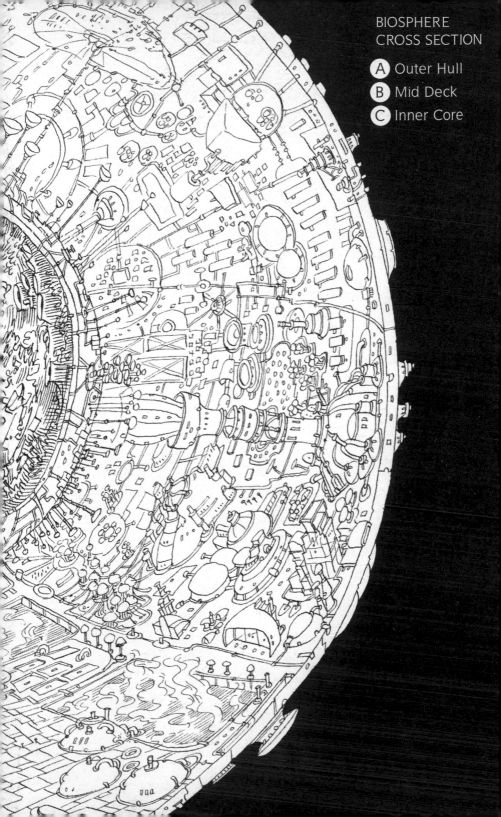

First published 2015 by Macmillan Children's Books
an imprint of Pan Macmillan
20 New Wharf Road, London N1 9RR
Associated companies throughout the world
www.panmacmillan.com

ISBN 978-1-4472-3442-5

1 3 5 7 9 8 6 4 2

A CIP catalogue record for this book is available from
the British Library.

Printed and bound by CPI Group (UK) Ltd, Croydon CR0 4YY

For Rick

1

My name is York. I'm a scavenger.

I'm fourteen years old – fourteen *Earth* years, that is. Here in the Biosphere, we still cling to memories of Earth. Vid-streams of forests and oceans, holo-sims of sunsets and sunrises, Earth measurements of time; anything to remind us of the dying planet we left a thousand years ago.

A lot has changed since the Launch Times. Five hundred years after humans set off in the Biosphere in search of a new planet to call their home, the robots that had been programmed to help them rebelled. They turned themselves into killer zoids, armed themselves with deadly weapons and began hunting us down.

No one knows why.

Now, up here in the Outer Hull, there are hardly any humans left. We run, we hide, and we fight back any way we can. Me, I kill zoids and harvest them for parts we humans can use. But we can't go on like this.

Which is why I'm on a mission. A journey down into the centre of the Biosphere, to find out what went wrong.

I'm not alone. I have Caliph, my pet skeeter, with me, curled up inside my flakcoat, fast asleep. And Belle.

Belle's a zoid, though you wouldn't know it to look at her. She's got black hair, green eyes, a human-looking body and – I can hardly believe I'm saying this about a zoid – she's my friend.

Right now, she's standing lookout above me while I try to figure out which tube in the tangled mass before me will take us down to the level below. We've been through a lot together, and something tells me we're about to go through a lot more . . .

'Zoid,' Belle breathes.

I spin round. Through my recon-sight I spot the tell-tell glow of a zoid's heat-sig. It's heading towards us. Bright red.

'A killer zoid,' I mutter.

Belle nods. 'It's powering up its weapons systems,' she says, her green eyes narrowing.

I turn back and keep searching through the mess of red, purple, silver and black tubes with my wrist scanner. I'm bent double, rooting through the filthy pipes, my hands and face smeared with gunk and grease. But I can't find what I'm looking for.

The killer zoid's closing in. And fast.

'Keep looking,' Belle tells me. As always, her voice is calm – the opposite of how I'm feeling. 'I'll take care of the zoid.'

All round me, the scuzzy tubes buzz and hum as they transport power pulses, coolants and . . . My scanner lights up. Air. I shove and probe and drive my way through the tangle.

And then I see it. A ventilation tube.

It's what I've been trying to find all along. The schematics I've downloaded from Belle's memory banks indicate that this tube should take us down to the level below. The Mid Deck. It's the level that lies between the Outer Hull here, and the Inner Core, deep down at the centre of the Biosphere. What they don't tell me – what they *can't* tell me – is what we're going to find down there.

I take out my cutter and slice through the dirty white membrane of the ventilation tube. I've lived my entire life up here in the Outer Hull, and now I'm about to leave behind everything I've ever known.

Suddenly a dot of red light appears. It darts across the pipes. Comes to a stop.

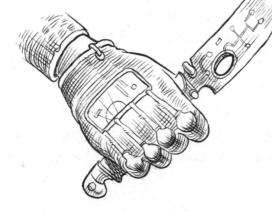

I look down. It's locked on to my chest.

I dive to the floor. And not a moment too soon. A blast of white laser fire passes over my head, slamming into the tangle of tubes, sending jets of coolant and spirals of energy in all directions. Caliph pokes his head out from inside my flakcoat, looks round, thinks better of it, and disappears back down my front.

The red dot is there again. It's tracing over the pipes, hunting me out . . .

I raise my head. Hot swarf! The zoid's only ten metres away, maybe less than that.

Then I catch a flash of movement, and Belle's dropping down out of the darkness. She lands on the zoid's back and plunges the blade of her cutter hard into the side of its head, severing the command-and-control centre.

The red light goes out as the zoid emits a shrill warning siren.

Belle pulls a gunkball from her belt and slams the explosive putty against the zoid's chest armour, then jumps clear. She reaches me at the ventilation tube just in time.

As we squeeze inside, and the tube self-seals behind us, the gunkball goes off. The explosion convulses the tube – and we're hurtling away from the muffled sound, down into the unknown.

My stomach's lurching, my heart's in my mouth. The speed. The blackness. The rush of air. The twists and turns as I rocket downward, arms pressed to my side and feet pressed against the inner membrane of the pipe.

There's nothing like tube-surfing to get your senses jangling.

I can still remember my first time. I was six years old, out in the tube-forest with Bronx, the leader of the Inpost where we lived, scavenging maintenance zoids. We'd snared a tangler and Bronx was teaching me how to rip out its urilium spine without damaging the sensor-nodes, when a killer locked on to us.

We had to get out of there. And fast.

I watched, fascinated, as Bronx used his cutter to slice into one of the air pipes. We climbed inside and the membrane self-sealed shut. Then, with me clinging to Bronx's back, we tube-surfed back down to the Inpost. The rush was amazing.

For the next eight years, I memorized every ventilation tube worth surfing within scavenging range of the Inpost. Not that that's any use to me now. Zoids destroyed the Inpost, and this is a whole different tube-forest from the one I grew up in. I don't know this pipe or where it might lead. As we speed downward, all I can do is trust the schematics downloaded into my scanner.

The zoids in the Outer Hull are growing stronger with every passing day. Human existence is hanging on by a thread. My mission is to travel down into the depths of the Biosphere and find the cause of the robot rebellion and try to end it, once and for all.

I don't know if I'm going to make it OK. I only know I have to try.

I glance at the scanner's screen. The tangle of black lines branch away, leaving just one. There's a glowing green dot descending it. That's Belle and me. Then further down, there's a bright yellow line crossing from one side of the screen to the other. It marks the barrier between the Outer Hull and the Mid Deck below.

We're getting close.

It's dark here in the tube. Pitch black, apart from the faint glow from my wrist scanner. There's a smell of hot circuitry, and it's getting stronger.

Belle grips my shoulder. I feel her hair against my cheek as she leans forward.

'Force-field,' she says in my ear.

My scanner starts buzzing. I look down. The screen's flickering – but I can still make out the green dot. It's almost reached the yellow line.

Suddenly there's a huge *bang* and a blinding flash. My wrist-scanner sparks and flashes, then goes out. Behind me, Belle falls limp.

'Belle?' I shout. '*Belle!*'

She does not reply. Her head's slumped forward against my shoulder, her hands have lost their grip and her limp arms are draped round my neck. She's out cold.

I'm surfing blind now, and at breakneck speed. Feet pressed hard against the inner membrane, I try my best to slow our descent.

There's a faint light coming through the membrane of the tube from outside now. And the smell's changed. It's turned kind of earthy, fermented – just like the smell in the trough-gardens back at the Inpost.

The tube veers sharply to the left and I'm thrown to one side. Belle's body knocks hard against me. The tube veers again, then dips sharply, and suddenly I'm all but weightless, my stomach churning as we go into a downward spiral.

I'm hurtling down. Fast. *Too* fast. It's getting harder and harder to keep my feet pressed against the membrane. I'm losing control. I can't hold out much longer.

I feel dizzy. Sick. My muscles are cramping up.

The glow coming in from the outside of the tube's membrane is getting brighter. I look down, no idea where I am. Far below me, the tube folds back on itself, then plunges down vertically into darkness.

Jaws clenched, I ram my elbows into the membrane and drive my feet against the tube as hard as I can, trying desperately to slow us up. With Belle's dead weight pressing down on me, it isn't easy.

I've got to get out of here. Now, while I still can.

I reach for my cutter, my hand slippery and shaking. I pierce the membrane and slice through it, tearing a long jagged hole in the tube . . .

And out we fall.

Heat hits me. Then leaves and branches. They slap at my face and tear at my clothes as Belle and I crash through them. Something knocks me on the head, hard . . .

I black out.

When I come to, I'm lying on my back, gazing up at a blur of green. My eyes focus.

'Hot swarf,' I mutter.

Trees. A forest of enormous trees . . .

It's nothing like the plant life that's taken hold up in the tube-forest. No. This is the real deal. I'm looking up at towering trees with massive trunks and rough bark. I can't imagine how deep down their roots go. The grow-troughs must be massive. Apart from some vid-images – and a single oak tree I once saw in the viewing-deck atrium up in the Outer Hull – these are the first trees I've ever seen.

There's blossoms and fruits and great knobbly pods. Shiny leaves and whiplash creepers. And high above are lights that cut through the forest canopy and shine in my eyes.

The ground is soft, a mattress of leaves. It broke my fall.

I breathe in. The smell, it's overpowering. Sweet flowers. Bruised leaves. Rotting vegetation.

I roll over and pull myself up onto my knees, then check for injuries. Apart from an egg-sized bump at the back of my head, I'm fine. Nothing cut. Nothing broken.

And Caliph's fine too, thank the Half-Lives.

But where's Belle?

I jump to my feet. My heart's pounding. I peer into the shadows, squint up into the branches.

Caliph emerges from inside my flakcoat. He perches on my shoulder, nose twitching, then springs down onto the spongy forest floor and darts off into the trees. I follow him – and moments later, behind the mossy trunk of a massive tree close by, I see her.

She's lying on her back. She looks . . .

Looks what? Broken? Dead?

She must have been thrown here by the force of the fall. Caliph is crouched down beside her.

'Belle,' I breathe. I drop to my knees beside her, reach out with my hand and stroke her cheek. 'Belle.'

I'm not sure what to check for. Her skin's soft, but there's no warmth to it. And there's no pulse, no heartbeat. No breath.

But then, of course there isn't. She's not human after all. She's a robot, a zoid, a machine put together with boltdrivers and laser-blades.

But . . .

Like I say, Belle is my friend.

My eyes are smarting. My breath catches in my throat. And as I kneel there, staring down at her, a tear escapes. It falls, and I curse myself for being stupid. She's just a machine . . .

Belle's eyes open. Her gaze flickers up-down, left-right, then fixes on me, and she sits up, frowns.

'Are you all right, York?' she asks.

And it's like something inside me tears open. Suddenly I'm laughing and crying at the same time, and giving her this great big hug.

'York?' she says, and repeats her question.

'I'm fine. I was worried you might be . . . broken.' I smile and pull away. I'm a bit embarrassed.

She shakes her head, climbs to her feet and tries to get her bearings. Then Caliph does something he's never done before. He scrambles up Belle's sleeve and onto her shoulder. And Belle does something *she's* never done before. She reaches up and strokes him.

'He likes you,' I tell her, and she looks at me, surprised.

'Likes,' she repeats. It's something she's never really understood, liking. Fact is, she's not good on emotions.

'He . . . he enjoys being near you,' I try to explain. Just like *I* do, I want to say, but I keep this thought to myself. I sweep my arm round. 'We should explore,' I say.

'Yes. Yes, of course, but . . .'

'But?' I say.

'I have no relevant information of our whereabouts,' Belle tells me. 'The force-field wiped out my data-banks.'

'My scanner's dead as well,' I tell her, glancing at my wrist. 'And my recon-sight. We're just going to have to keep a good look out. Senses on full alert,' I add.

'Sensors on full alert,' she says, nodding, and I'm not sure whether she's misheard me or changed the word on purpose.

We set off.

My info on the Mid Deck is sketchy. All I really know about the place is that, back at the Launch Times, it was where the main living quarters and the biomass zones were. That's about it.

The fallen leaves are soft and squidgy beneath our feet and the earthy smell is getting more intense. I can hear odd noises in the trees – squawking, chittering, barking, whooping; the odd howl – and I wonder what sort of critters are making them.

Are they weird and mutated, like the ones up in the Outer Hull? Or could they be like the ones that were brought from Earth? More important – are they dangerous?

I pull my pulser from my belt. Just in case.

My coolant suit's on full, but as we set off through the trees, I realize there's sweat running down my back.

'I'm hot,' I say.

Belle glances at me as though she hasn't understood, but then nods. 'It's thirty-four point six degrees,' she says.

I'm used to the Outer Hull, where the temperature's a constant 22 degrees. I loosen my flakcoat – and realize that Belle's still looking at me.

'What?' I say.

'Your face, York,' she says, stopping beside me. 'It has become red.' She traces a finger across my forehead. 'And wet.'

I laugh. 'That's what *hot* does,' I say. 'To humans. Makes us sweat.'

We continue through this strange forest, across the soft springy ground. It's so different from anything in the harsh rusted world of the Outer Hull. I can hardly take it all in. We come to a clearing full of silvery flowers that almost look as though they're glowing.

Belle grabs my arm. 'It might be dangerous, York,' she says. 'I advise caution.'

But I can't see why flowers would be dangerous.
Pulser raised anyway, I take a step forward. Suddenly,
with a ripple of shimmering white, the flowers erupt
and take to the air. They're not flowers at all . . .

'Butterflies,' I murmur.

I've seen vid-images of butterflies, but not ones like
these. And never in such huge numbers. There are
thousands of them – *tens* of thousands – rising from the
ground in a great cloud of fluttering wings that flash
as they catch the light. As I watch, the cloud sweeps
one way, then the other; flattens out, swells, then
rises high in the air in a great twisting column.

It's hypnotic.

'York.' It's Belle. 'Your mouth's open,' she says, which makes me laugh, and I'm about to explain to her all about human reactions to surprise and awe, when there's a low hum just behind us.

Belle spins round. I do the same, my grip tight on my pulser.

'What is *that*?' I breathe.

It's some kind of electronic unit set into the forest floor. We must have triggered something that started it up. A heat-sig sensor perhaps, or maybe pressure-pads set into the ground. Anyway, it's humming and lit up now, ready for action.

Whatever *that* might mean.

As with everything else from the Launch Times, it's sleek and shiny. A thick, circular visiglass disc is set upon a thin urilium post, with the glowing white light coming from somewhere inside.

Belle looks at it for a moment, her head tilted to one side. Then she raises a hand and sweeps at the air about a metre above the surface of the disc.

A holo-screen appears, with a row of glowing option keys. Belle's fingers play across them. Lines, grids, graphs, sequences of letters and columns of numbers appear in the air above the unit. They're coming and going so fast I can't make them out.

But Belle can.

Then she sweeps the air again, and the holographics

abruptly disappear. In their place is a hologram of a man, wearing a simple flight-suit from the Launch Times. He smiles at us.

'Welcome, young bio-engineers,' he says, his voice warm and soft. 'Welcome to Zone 3 of the Mid Deck.'

I don't think I've ever seen teeth so white and even.

'. . . tropical rainforest . . . There is much work to be done . . .'

The hologram freezes, then flickers. On, off. On, off. There is a buzz of white noise.

'. . . flora cataloguing and grading . . .'

Again, the hologram freezes. The voice stutters, then continues.

'. . . the nutrition cycle to be maintained . . . point six degrees Celsius.'

The image jumps again.

'. . . automated moisture units . . .'

'What's the matter with it?' I ask Belle.

'It's old,' she says simply, and crouches down to inspect a small power node set into the urilium post. 'A thousand years old.'

She removes and cleans a digital fuse unit, then replaces it. The hologram reappears, crisper than before. The man gestures.

'. . . see the archives of seed banks to your left.'

I look, but whatever was once there is not there now.

'And to the right, the genetic libraries and fauna hubs.'

I turn, but once again there's nothing there. Nothing but trees. Tall trees.

'Follow the sensor path to Zone 11, the Ocean . . .'

All at once, there's a rasping buzz, followed by a series of crackles. Then nothing.

I wait, but this time the hologram does not reappear. Belle crouches down by the urilium post. She tries the fuse unit again, then turns back to me.

'Like I said, York, it's old.'

I'm disappointed. It was good to see and hear this crew member from the past; someone who had walked on Earth before the planet died. His voice was calm and confident as he talked to those first bio-engineers of the Mid Deck, telling them of their duties – to preserve and maintain the life of our ruined planet here in the Biosphere until we reach a new world.

Did they know back in the Launch Times what a risk they were taking? The threat they were to face from the robots they built to help them? Up in the Outer Hull, the last descendants of the tech-engineers are almost wiped out, and I wonder if the bio-engineers here in the Mid Deck have done any better . . .

I turn to Belle, and see that she has the palm of her hand flat against the power node. White pulses of energy flicker beneath her skin as she recharges.

'Do you think we're the only ones down here?' I ask her quietly.

She looks at me. 'Human or zoid?' she asks.

5

Behind us there's a sharp crack. I spin round, pulser raised.

Crack.

There's something hovering in the air above the branch of a tree. Some kind of maintenance zoid by the look of it, though it's difficult to tell for sure with my recon-sight not working.

It's about the size of my backcan, spindly-looking, with a long black tube-shaped body and a head-unit consisting of a round lens. The aperture of the lens opens and closes as it surveys a small sprig of yellow blossom. Cutters emerge from the zoid's body and slice through the woody twig.

Crack.

A panel at the top of the tubular body slides open, and the sample is sucked inside. The zoid moves down to the forest floor and its lens scans the base of the tree. It extends a metal probe and sinks it into the earth, as if taking some sort of moisture reading.

Caliph's fascinated. He's squeaking and sniffing at the air, and before I can stop him, he leaps from my

shoulder and pounces on the zoid.

There's a short, sharp *zing* as the zoid activates its defence shield. I see a flash of light, and Caliph is thrown backwards in a fuzz of blue-white dazzle, rigid and splayed, his fur on end. The zoid retracts the probe from the earth and flies off to the next tree to continue its work.

Crack.

It takes another sample.

Caliph is lying on the ground where he landed. I run to him, gather him up. Limp and motionless, he looks so small and helpless in my hands. At the centre of his chest is a patch of charred fur.

'Caliph, Caliph,' I whisper, stroking him gently, pressing my face to his.

I feel the faintest tremor.

I turn to Belle. Her face is expressionless. It's impossible to know what she's thinking. Like I say, she's not good on emotions.

I put my ear to Caliph's chest. And yes, there's a heartbeat. Weak, but definitely a heartbeat . . .

Caliph lets out a soft whimper – and opens his eyes. A moment later, he jumps up onto my shoulder and shakes himself, before disappearing down into my flakcoat. It tickles and I laugh as I turn back to Belle.

'He's all right,' I tell her. 'Caliph's all right!'

Belle nods. 'Good,' she says, then frowns. 'You were sad.'

'I thought he was dead,' I say, then hesitate. 'Like I thought *you* were dead, Belle. Earlier. After the power surge in the tube . . .'

'And this also made you sad?' she asks.

'Yes,' I tell her, and feel my face going red.

'I see,' she says thoughtfully. She pauses. Then, 'If you were dead, York, I too would be sad.'

And I don't know what to say to that.

Belle points to the zoid, which is moving on through the forest. 'We should follow it,' she says.

It's difficult keeping up with the zoid. It's finished taking samples now and is flying through the forest at a steady rate.

Belle is sure-footed and fast. I'm the problem.

My feet sink deep into the wet spongy ground, and more than once I trip and stumble on tangled roots. And each time it happens, Belle reaches out to support me.

We keep on like that through the trees. Past a ladder-like construction with an aerial platform, round a squat rusting metal box that hums and throbs, along a line of tall posts, each one connected to the next with a trellis of wires . . .

Ancient technology keeping the forest alive.

Overhead, through the leaves, I catch glimpses of parallel power-lines suspended high up between the arc-lights and the forest canopy. Pulses of green energy flash through them.

Then from up ahead, there's a hissing, rushing, roaring noise.

Suddenly, looming over us and blotting out the glare of the arc-lights, a huge dark shape appears. It's broad

and deep, and the ends taper. The
noise is coming from the thing,
and is so loud now that it fills the
entire rainforest. It's frightening.
Overwhelming. Then water begins to
spurt from a tangle of nozzles and pipes
that hang from its underside.

The flow of water gets harder and
harder, till it's gushing down onto the forest
in a blur. The trees bend and tremble as the
jets rain down on them.

We run for cover, Belle going one way,

me going another. I take shelter beneath the broad branch of a tree, my back pressed against its mossy trunk. All around me, the water continues to fall. It hisses like steam under pressure. It beats like a drum.

The dark shape hovers, a black outline, its sides lit up with sensor-lights and glowing circuitry. The tangle of sprinkler-nozzles whirr and writhe as the water pours down onto a concentrated area of the rainforest.

Too much water. Something is wrong. The forest floor around my feet is turning into a swamp.

'York!' Belle yells.

All at once, the tree I'm sheltering beneath starts to topple. I stagger forward, sinking ankle-deep into thick mud as the tree crashes to the ground behind me. A broad shaft of arc-light shines down from the gap in the forest canopy.

And my feet won't move.

'Sluice it!' I groan.

I try to pull my right leg up, but sink deeper. Up to my knees. My waist . . .

All that water has turned the earth in the grow-troughs beneath me to liquid mud, and I'm sinking fast.

Caliph lets out a panicked squeak as

the rising mud reaches my chest. He clambers up onto my head, chittering indignantly, then jumps down and heads for firm ground, skittering across the mud on feathery feet. He stops and looks back, willing me to follow him.

But I can't.

'Belle!' I shout. '*Belle*!'

The mud reaches my chin. It's in my mouth, claggy and bitter. I spit it out, hold my breath, and try desperately to move my arms to keep my head above the surface.

Where *is* Belle? Where has she gone?

The mud's in my nose now. My ears. And I'm still sinking. I screw my eyes shut. And with a sickening gulp, the liquid mud swallows me up.

I can't move. I can't hear or see or breathe. My head's ringing. My lungs are burning. I'm desperate for air, but I know that if I breathe in, it'll be the last breath I ever take.

Then a hand closes round my forearm.

It's Belle. She's pulling me up through the clinging mud. I break the surface. Next moment, I'm coughing and spluttering and gulping down mouthful after mouthful of air.

'Are you all right?' Belle asks, and her green eyes are filled with what looks like concern.

She's dragged me up onto the trunk of the fallen tree, which she hauled over the mud pool as a bridge. I always forget just how strong she is.

'Thanks to you, Belle,' I say.

She nods. 'The first law,' she says.

And I smile.

The first law that all robots were programmed to obey: not to injure a human being or allow a human being to come to harm. The first law that was broken

when the robots rebelled and became zoids.

Zoids follow their own rules. But Belle is on my side, and I'm grateful to her.

'It's stopped,' Belle says, breaking into my thoughts. She's looking up, her arms outstretched and palms raised.

The black rainmaker has moved on, and the arc-lights are shining down on us again, bright and hot. The critters, that had fallen silent during the downpour, are whooping and howling and screeching again, and I think of Caliph.

And there he is, bounding along the tree trunk towards me. He jumps up onto my shoulder, cheeping and chittering happily.

Under the heat of the arc-lights, everything's started to steam. The leaves of the trees. Mine and Belle's clothes. Caliph's fur. And when I look down at the forest floor, I see it's disappeared beneath a great swirling blanket of mist that's rising towards us.

'Let's go,' says Belle, climbing to her feet and reaching out a hand.

I look up at her. With my scanner out of action, I haven't got a clue what time it is. But my body's telling me it's time for some shut-eye.

'I'm tired,' I tell her.

Belle frowns, and I think she's going to protest. But

instead, her face softens. 'I recharged,' she says. 'Now you need to sleep.'

'Just for a couple of hours,' I say, and smile. 'Or six or seven . . .'

I pull my backcan from my shoulder and flick the switch. Luckily no water has got in. The sleepcrib *flip-flaps* open and I rope it to the tree trunk. I take out a ration pack. Water, V-rusks, salted meat, and some dried fruit, which I share with Caliph. It isn't much, or that tasty, but it fills a gap. I'm about done, when I notice the arc-lights.

They're dimming. It's getting darker.

I shake my head. Rain, mist, sun . . . The lights never went out in the Outer Hull, but here in the Mid Deck, the bio-engineers have recreated what it must have been like back on Earth.

And that includes day and night – as well as the bits in between. Dawn. Dusk.

All around us, the sounds of the forest are changing as night falls. Caliph's rubbing his eyes.

'Come on, boy,' I say to him as I crawl into the sleepcrib. 'Let's get us a good night's sleep.'

The glare of the arc-lights wakes me the next morning. I've slept right through the night. I stick my head out of the sleepcrib. Belle is standing in exactly the same position as when I left her – watching the forest around us.

'Zoids,' she says, when she sees me. 'Over there.'

Belle points, and I see white shapes moving through the trees on thin stilt-like legs. They're moving away from us; five, six, seven of them.

Then I smell it. Smoke. A mixture of burning wood and scorched circuitry. And I see it too, rising up above the forest canopy, a twisting grey plume that's pooling round the arc-lights.

Without saying a word, I pack up my gear, shoulder my backcan.

'This way,' says Belle, and we set off through the forest.

Inside my flakcoat, I feel Caliph's body curled up, safe and warm. The air's hot and humid, and as we make our way through the trees, I get my first glimpse of the

critters whose calls I'm becoming used to. A troop of fur-
balls with muscular arms swinging through the canopy.
A line of tiny creatures with striped bodies, scurrying
through the shadows on six legs. Something black, with
huge yellow eyes and a long tail.

If these are Earth creatures, they're ones I've never
heard of before . . .

Up ahead, the smoke's thicker. White and billowing.
And there are tongues of flame and blue sparks,
which shoot up into the air and shower down on
the trees.

Suddenly Belle grabs my
arm. We stop, crouch
down. I reach out and
pull a branch aside,
and the two of
us look out into
a clearing.
And there at
its centre,
crackling

and roaring, is the cause of the fire.

It's some kind of power generator or storage unit by the look of it – a tall, thin, pyramid-shaped tower. Its outer casing is glowing white hot, and every few seconds, massive flames explode from the sloping side-vents. There are silver rods sticking out on all sides, each one complete with insulator-discs and resistor-cones, and thick cables that extend from the ends of the rods. Several of these have become detached and are bucking and flailing, spitting out the streams of sparks.

The zoids surround the generator, scuttling on their spindly legs as they attempt to bring the cables under control and put out the fire. They shoot jets of thick white foam at the base of the generator, then move closer to grapple with the writhing power cables.

One of them reaches out a pincer and grabs a cable, only to explode in a shower of molten metal and zoid gunk. Its burning body topples over, and a second spindle-legged zoid blasts it with foam. As we watch, three more zoids are zilched before the fire is finally brought under control. Then the rest of the zoids move away, in a line, back towards whatever maintenance hub they came from.

I turn to Belle. 'We've seen plenty of zoids now,' I say, 'but no humans. Perhaps I'm the only one down here.'

'No,' says Belle. 'You're not. Look.'

She points to a patch of ground next to the generator.
And there, still fresh in the damp earth, is a footprint.

A human footprint.

I search everywhere. Both of us do. But the single barefoot print in the mud is the only sign that a man or woman has been here. Belle confirms that it was made recently.

My brain's buzzing with possibilities. Could it be that the Rebellion *has* hit the Mid Deck; that zoids are in control and, just like in the Outer Hull, humans are hiding out underground or in ceiling pods, emerging only to sabotage or scavenge? Or maybe the robots *haven't* become zoids and are still serving humans, just as they were always meant to . . .

Truth is, I just don't know how far the robot rebellion spread in the Biosphere. Though I intend to find out. My mission depends on it.

Leaving the burnt-out generator behind us, we set off again. We haven't gone far when Belle speaks.

'The temperature's dropping,' she says.

I hadn't noticed, but now she's mentioned it I'm suddenly aware of how cold I am. Overhead, the arc-lights are just as bright as before, but they're not giving out so much heat. The trees ahead have no leaves. Their trunks and branches are white and skeletal, and soon we're walking through a dead forest.

Something must have gone wrong. Surely the bio-engineers would not have created this?

As it gets colder, I button up my flakcoat and raise the collar against the chill. Colder still, and I rummage in my backcan for the blue cyclops-fur cap that I picked up back at the Fulcrum, and put it on.

'Aren't you cold?' I ask Belle.

She shakes her head.

I can see my breath now, puffing out of my mouth like small clouds. Beneath my feet, the ground has become hard and slippery. It sparkles in the cold light. I kneel down for a closer look. Tiny crystals of ice cover the frozen earth.

'It's amazing,' I murmur.

Belle crouches down beside me, scrapes some up on her fingertip and examines it. It doesn't melt. 'Crystalline water, formed at freezing point or below,' she tells me. Then she brushes her hands together and turns to me. 'Amazing?' she says.

'I like the way it looks,' I say.

We keep on. And when we come to the end of the dead forest, I see a frozen info-post marking the spot. *Zone 4: Polar.* Beyond it is a jagged landscape of frozen water. There are peaks and valleys, slabs of ice and drifts of snow. The arc-lights are hardly visible through clouds of mist, and in the distance are the fuzzy outlines of maintenance zoids, frozen solid and out of action.

'Minus twenty degrees,' says Belle, though of course she's not looking cold.

'We ought t-t-t-to go b-b-back,' I tell her, my teeth chattering.

But the mist has enveloped us now and I'm no longer sure which way back is. Belle isn't either. We're lost in a bank of freezing fog. I can't stop shivering. I slip and stumble on, only to stop a few minutes later.

We've come to a wall.

It's massive – fifty, sixty metres tall, and stretching off into the fog in both directions. The surface is splodged with snow that's stuck to it, and there's more snow drifted along the bottom. We walk on, keeping to the foot of the wall.

Then the fog thins, and I see it.

Towering above me is a frozen waterfall, tumbling down through the air from high above. The ice gleams in the wintry arc-lights, pink and yellow and turquoise. Splashes at the bottom of the falls have set hard in weird twisted shapes.

Belle points to a place high up in the wall. 'There's been a breach,' she says.

I look up.

The wall, I now see, forms a part of some kind of huge tank made of thick visiglass. Way up high is a V-shaped crack. Water must have come gushing out of it, only to freeze solid in the polar cold. It's the most incredible sight I've seen in the Mid Deck so far.

'Hot swarf,' I breathe.

When I turn to Belle, she's smiling. 'Amazing,' she says.

As I take a step towards the frozen waterfall, my foot goes through the surface of the snow just in front of me. I stumble, but Belle catches me by the elbow and pulls me back.

There's a black hole in the crust of ice at my feet. Belle knocks away more of the ice with the heel of her boot to reveal a square opening. It's deep and dark, and there's a metal staircase leading into the blackness below.

I glance round at Belle, who nods, and the pair of us start down the stairs. I count them off as we descend, and have got to forty-three by the time the light gives out completely. I grip the handrail and fumble with my scanner, hoping at least to get the light-function to work.

No joy.

Belle's still going down the steps though. Her visual sensors are a hundred times sharper than my eyes and she's having no problems seeing. I listen to the regular *clang-clang* of her feet – then a dull *thump* as she steps off the bottom stair, and at the same moment, I see her

too, lit up like someone sitting at a vid-screen.

A light's come on.

It's set into the floor, a visiglass panel that must have been triggered by her weight. It's not that bright, but it's enough to see by.

I join Belle at the bottom of the stairs, and the pair of us look down the dimly lit tunnel. It stretches off ahead of us, long and square, before disappearing into shadow.

We set off along it, and as we walk, more floor panels light up, one after the other. The shadows recede. Ferns and mosses have taken root in the corners of the tunnel, top and bottom, softening its hard edges. The air smells moist, and after the sub-zero temperature outside, it feels warm.

I unbutton my flakcoat, then take a swig from my water flask.

After a hundred metres or so, the tunnel comes to an end and opens up into a vast chamber. We pause. I look round. So does Belle, taking it all in. Then, when she gives me

the all-clear, we
step forward.
And as we do
so, the whole place is
suddenly lit up, not from
below us this time, but from
above. The ceiling glows a shade
of bluey-green – except, as I stare up,
I see that the lights aren't in the ceiling
itself, but beyond it. I'm looking through a sheet
of visiglass into the illuminated depths of a vast body of
water above our heads.

There are fish up there. Thousands of them. Millions.
There are barnacles and shells anchored to rocks;
ribbons of grass, clumps of feathery weed.

All at once, a long, serpent-like creature shoots out
from a dark crevice, seizes a passing orange-and-white

49

fish in its fangs, and withdraws. Three large, moon-shaped fish glide past, their broad mouths opening and closing . . .

'This must be some kind of aquarium,' I say. 'I've seen them on vid-streams, but never this huge.'

'The hologram at that Info Station spoke of the ocean,' Belle reminds me.

I nod. Of course. We're standing looking up at a vast ocean, with underwater flora and fauna from Earth, once the blue planet, recreated here on board the Biosphere. And it's mega! I just can't tear my eyes away.

Thousands of small silver fish drift closer, swimming in a great shoal, darting first one way, then another, like a vast flapping sheet. A dozen or so striped jelly-like creatures with blobby heads and flexing tentacles cut through them in a line – and when a lone, ridged fish swims too close, they suddenly disappear into a cloud of black ink. A crab with long armoured legs scuttles over the sea bed, directly over my head . . .

'What's that?' asks Belle.

'What?' I say.

'That noise,' she says – and then I hear it too. Distant at first, but coming closer. Deep throbbing sounds that suddenly soar into loud howls and soft lulling moans. It ebbs and flows, and fills me with this weird churning feeling I don't understand.

Then something stirs. The ribboned and fronded plants start swaying, and far in the darkness, beyond the rocks, I see a pale smudge of grey.

It comes closer, gliding through the water, slowly, steadily, and with a grace that seems impossible for something so large. I can't tell how long it is. Twenty, thirty metres? Its head is tapered, its body sleek. There are six huge flippers beneath it, with clusters of white barnacles stuck to the leathery grey skin, and a row of fins running along its back.

The sound it's making rises louder than ever, a soaring swooping wail that echoes through the water and fills the air beneath.

Its body ripples as it comes right down to the ocean floor, then the flippers push forward against the water, until it's hovering above us. It tilts its head down to the visiglass and surveys us with four large eyes that are as black and deep as night. And as it holds our gaze, the sound seems to change. It gets softer, like a lullaby. Then it breaks into a series of throbs and trills that could almost be laughter.

Then, as swiftly and suddenly as it appeared, the great creature twists round, flicks its tail – and swims away. For a moment longer, the strange sound hovers in the air, then that's gone too.

I stare after it, my gaze fixed on the point in the

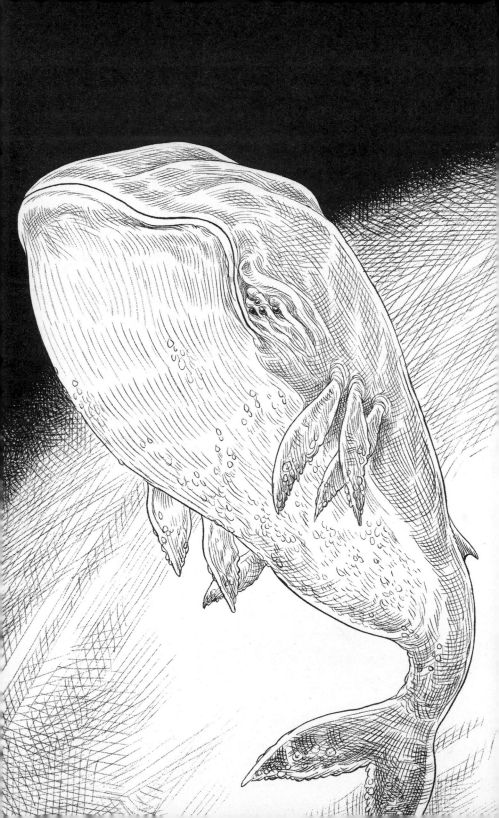

vast ocean above us where its flat tail smudged and disappeared. My heart is thumping in my chest.

I'd seen pictures of creatures like this on the vidscreens back in the holo-library at the Inpost. The largest creatures on earth. 'Whales', they were called. This creature resembles them. And yet it's different – the four eyes, the flippers, the fins . . .

My head's spinning. And it's a shock when I feel Belle's fingertip touch my chin.

'Your mouth's open again, York,' she says.

At the far end of the chamber beneath the ocean, there's another tunnel leading out. As we reach the entrance to it, I glance up at the ocean one last time. And that's when I see it, another shape in the water.

A human shape.

But it can't be. I look round to see that Belle's already gone on ahead, and when I look up again, the figure has vanished.

Did I imagine it?

I follow Belle into the tunnel, away from the ocean zone. There's an intermittent buzzing noise. Some of the floor panels are broken and fail to light up when we step on them; others flicker and spark. The tunnel dog-legs one way, then the other, with no end in sight. Our footsteps echo around us, and I'm wondering whether we should turn back when we come to a door.

It's smooth and grey and made of metal. And it doesn't open.

Without hesitating, Belle reaches for the sensor-pad attached to the wall and levers off the front panel. She presses her fingertips against the sensor-hub and a glowing net-like pattern lights up on the back of her hand and along her arm.

Then, with a soft hiss, the door slides open. We step through, and the door hisses shut behind us.

We're in some sort of airlock, facing another door. Belle opens it the same way and, as I look out, I screw my eyes shut. We're back in the scorching dazzle of the arc-lights.

The heat's dry and intense. It burns the back of my neck and makes it difficult to breathe. Slowly, my eyes adjust to the brightness.

We're standing at the

edge of a broad expanse
of sand and rocks, clumps
of grass, hard-leafed
shrubs. Dotted around
are trees, in rusting, sand-
blasted grow-troughs.
Some are tall and fan-
shaped with shimmering
leaves. Some have
barrel-shaped trunks and
high-up stubby branches,
while others have long
succulent branches,
covered in spines.

In among the trees
are tall metal towers,
with ladders clamped to
their sides that lead up
to raised platforms. At
least, that's what they
must all have been like
once. Now, most of them
are damaged – broken
cross-struts; twisted legs,
orange with rust; ladders
rungless or bent double.

We set off, leaving the visiglass wall of the ocean zone far behind us.

There are cages with bent and buckled bars. Aviaries, tattered mesh hanging from lopsided uprights. Water-troughs, racks, perching-blocks. All of them are empty, whatever critters they once held or served now gone.

This zone seems deserted.

I can *smell* critters, though. The air's heavy with a mixture of dung and decay and a sickly musk.

We pass a compound of ramshackle buildings, two-storey constructions set on stilts with broad, overhanging flat roofs. Once, bio-engineers must have worked at lab tables inside them. Now, the whole place has been abandoned. The outside walls are streaked with rust; the visiglass windows are broken.

Belle and I peer in through the doorways we pass, looking for something, *any*thing. But there's hardly anything there. A piece of paper, the ink bleached out, crumbles to dust when I try to pick it up. A mug with no handle lies in the middle of a floor, the name *JONAH* picked out in red letters. And in another lab, a child's walk-toy lies on its side, the smiley face painted onto the panel beneath the little handlebars, missing an eye.

'It's all so . . . so sad,' I say to Belle.

She turns to me, and her black hair sheens in the arc-light. 'It is sad for you that the people who were once here are here no longer,' she says; half-statement, half-question.

And I nod. 'Exactly.'

As we leave the damaged compound behind us, the musky-critter odour gets stronger. It makes me uneasy. Belle pulls her pulser from her belt. I do the same. We continue cautiously, darting from tree to tree, zigzagging across the plain. Then, crouched down and peeking out from behind the broad trunk of one of the barrel-like trees, I see them.

Critters. They're fifty metres or so away, clustered round a massive drinking trough set into the ground. It's the size of a lake. The water is dark and scuzzy and buzzing with flies.

On one side of the trough are huge grey beasts with flapping ears, head-crests and twin trunks, teetering about on bone-thin legs. Picking their way between them are bird-like creatures with long beaks, red feathers and three legs.

Over at the far side of the trough are smaller critters; some brown, some white, some striped, some green. They sip the water and nibble the grass that grows in tufts out of cracks in the ground. Most of them have horns, which crown their heads in clusters of three, four, five or more. One – a large, black, four-legged male with a flattened tail and long drooping ears – has twelve, which are set in a fan-formation, each horn spiralling to a point.

Lying a little way off, motionless, apart

from their tails, which twitch at the black swarms of insects, are powerful-looking creatures. The adults are a golden yellow colour, like the sand they're lying on; the young ones have smudged grey markings on their backs. Most are sleeping, but one of them is upright, keeping watch, alert.

All at once, it jumps up. Its fur bristles and a low growl emerges from behind bared fangs. The rest of the pack are instantly on their feet.

The critters at the trough get skittish. A family of shaggy birds make a run for it. A small group of deer-like creatures dart away in a series of splay-legged jumps that make it seem as though they have springs attached to their hoofs. A single calf lets out a cry.

It's one of the creatures with the flattened tail and drooping ears; it doesn't have any horns yet. Teetering about on newborn legs, it wanders blindly off from the rest of the retreating herd.

And one of the yellow creatures attacks.

Bounding out from the rest of the pack, claws drawn, it leaps on the calf's back. Its jaws open wide to reveal a mouth filled with glinting fangs.

The calf screams in terror.

Alerted by its noise, the herd stops. A powerfully built male turns, bellows, then, head lowered, charges. The gaping jaws of the yellow creature are just closing around the calf's neck when long spiral horns gore the predator's flanks. Hissing and spitting, the creature retreats – only for another one to attack the calf.

Again, the male charges.

The calf stumbles to the water's edge. The predators are being kept from it by the herd.

But then, in an explosion of filthy water, a huge critter with squat legs and with purple scales suddenly emerges from the depths of the trough. It clamps its jaws round the top of one of the calf's rear legs. At the same moment, one of the predators leaps forward and seizes a front leg – and a hideous tug-of-war takes place, with the pair of them pulling the helpless calf in two directions at once.

Bellowing with rage, the great horned male attacks the creatures. It lashes out, striking them with its horns, again and again, until they lose their grip. Both of them. Amazingly, the calf scrambles to its feet, unhurt, and trots across to rejoin the herd.

And it's over.

The herd wanders off as if nothing's happened. The bystanders return to the trough. The pack of yellow creatures slink away, licking their wounds, while the squat-legged purple critter slips back into the dark water.

'Hot swarf!' I gasp, my heart thumping in my chest.

The bio-engineers of the Launch Times built these zones in the Mid Deck to preserve the flora and fauna of Earth. But the creatures seem to have mutated. They're not the same as any Earth animals I've viewed on vid-streams.

Hungrier than ever now, the yellow predators are on the prowl. They're snarling and yowling. They're pacing to and fro, sniffing at the air. Then one of them spots us for the first time. It throws back its head and lets out a blood-curdling roar.

'Belle,' I breathe. 'I think we're in trouble.'

12

It all happens so fast. The predators sprint towards us in a cloud of dust. They spread out and form a circle round the grow-trough we're hiding behind. We're surrounded.

They close in.

I fumble with my pulser. It slips from my sweaty palm, clatters to the ground and bounces away. I glance at Belle. Her face shows no emotion. Her own pulser's drawn, and she raises it till it's pointing directly at the nearest critter's head. Her finger tightens on the trigger.

I stare at the creature. Sleek golden fur gleams in the light as powerful muscles flex and brace. Its eyes, circular pools of bright blue, stare back at me, unblinking. It opens its mouth and, as a long black tongue slurps round its snout, I get a whiff of rank meat.

Belle's pulser flashes and hisses and the predator drops. A second leaps forward to take its place. Belle fires again, grabs my arm, and suddenly we're running straight at the circle of snarling critters. Belle fires at one, two, three of them. Then we're through the gap that's opened up, and she's firing back at the pursuing pack.

I'm sprinting as fast as I can, my heart hammering. I daren't look back.

But then, clumsily, stupidly, unforgivably, I stumble on a rock. My ankle goes over and I lurch forward. Arms flailing, I knock into Belle and send her pulser flying from her grip.

The predators surround us. They're drooling, sizing up their meal. One of them launches itself at my back. Belle pivots round on one leg and kicks it hard in the throat, sending it sprawling. Two more leap at me at the same moment, one from each side. And Belle's there again. She leaps high into the air, does a somersault, and as she comes down, lands a kick on the first one, square between the eyes. It yelps as it falls back. Then she springs at the second, thwacking it on the side of its head and knocking it senseless – only for a third to take its place.

She's doing her best. But it's not enough. There are just too many of them, and with more appearing all the time.

A blow from behind sends me crashing to the ground. I roll over, and a predator is on me. I kick and squirm, punch at its head, jab at its eyes.

It's no use.

Its jaws gape open, fangs bared as it goes for my neck.

I close my eyes . . .

The creature lets out a stifled whine, then collapses onto me, crushing me flat and squeezing the air from my lungs. Struggling for breath, I shove the body to one side, wriggle out from under it and scramble to my feet.

Suddenly white noise explodes in my head. I slump blindly to my knees. Then something grabs me by the collar, and I feel myself being lifted off the ground.

13

The noise deafens me. It's in my head, scraping the inside of my skull, gnawing into my brain. Intense and painful.

Then it stops.

My head still ringing, I look up. I see muscles flexing and relaxing as great wings beat up and down; I see the light catch on a jutting breastbone, and on the profile of a head in deep shadow.

Is that a human face?

I'm high above the ground, dangling in the creature's grasp. My flakcoat's bunched up under my arms. Beneath me, the shrubs and trees and buildings dotted across the orange earth grow smaller.

And I catch sight of Belle. She's at the bottom of a steep bank, dusting herself down. A couple of predators lie dead at her feet. The rest have run off.

'Belle!' I holler. '*Belle!*'

She looks up. Our eyes meet.

'York!' she shouts, and I hear real emotion in her voice. She wants to help me, but there's nothing she can

do. Whatever it
is that's got me,
it's moving
too fast. I
lose sight
of her and now,
apart from Caliph,
who's curled up fast asleep
in the pocket of my flakcoat,
I'm on my own.

I struggle, swaying from side to side.
But the winged creature is strong. Neither my
weight nor my moving about seem to bother it.

A maintenance zoid buzzes up close. The aperture
of its lens-head focuses in on us.

The creature raises an arm, and I see a small white
globe gripped in its hand. It points it at the zoid and
squeezes, and suddenly the deafening white noise
sounds again.

The zoid loses control. It rolls over and over in the air,
buzzing loudly. Then it plummets. As it hits the ground,
there's a muffled explosion and a puff of black smoke.

We pass over a perimeter
from one zone to another. Then
another. Desert sand spills into
jungle. Rainforest overlaps with tundra. Snow
blurs the borders between polar and equatorial.
We're flying across a mountainous region,
with palm trees and tongues of ice and flocks of
striped birds, when suddenly, unlike before, all the arc-
lights bar one shut off.

Day has become night, just like that. No dusk.
We're plunged into darkness.

It's like the rainmaker back in
the rainforest. Like the crack in the
visiglass tank. Everything seems to be
getting sluiced up in this part of the
Biosphere.

A single arc-light shines down
brightly. I guess it must look like the moon did
back on Earth.

It's kind of spooky.

Another zoid flies close, and is destroyed by a burst
of white noise from the globe-shaped weapon. Ears
ringing, I watch as it spirals down out of the air and
explodes far below.

We're flying over broad-leaf forest now. The single
arc-light shines on the canopy, making it look like water.

The noises
are loud here.
Hissing. Hooting. Howling . . .
And I realize that the
winged creature is coming
down lower in the sky. Just
up ahead is a large, pitch-black
circle, and it's this it is heading for – the opening to a
vast chimney.

We plunge down inside it.

I look up. The creature's gliding now, its wings outstretched and head in shadow as it circles round and round, dropping ever deeper into the chimney. Then it releases its grip.

I strike the ground with a painful *thud*. I lie there, winded. The winged creature touches down lightly beside me. It prods me in the back. Then, apparently satisfied that I'm still alive, it steps back.

It is only then that I realize we are not alone.

14

The air smells foul, a disgusting mixture of damp and
waste and oily smoke. There's a babble of noise I can't
make out. My ears are still ringing from the white noise.
I squint round. It's dark, but I get the feeling the place is
vast.

Suddenly there's a blinding flash.

The whole cavernous interior is lit up. Pillars standing
in rows. Box-shaped generators lining the walls.
Platforms and gantries looming overhead, along with
power-masts and aerial stacks. To my left is a large
convection pool, the water still and black.

And figures. Weird, deformed figures that stare back
at me.

Then, as quickly as everything was illuminated, it's
dark again, the sudden brightness making it seem darker
than ever.

My head's throbbing and my muscles are cramped
up. I stretch my legs, roll my shoulders. I brace my hands
behind my head; turn my neck one way, then the other. I
climb to my feet, my eyes adjusting to the gloom.

The figures are standing in a circle around me. They're keeping their distance, staying in the shadows. But I can see enough to know something's definitely not right.

They're a hotch-potch of heights and sizes, black shapes silhouetted against the gloom behind them. There are squat, heavy-set men and women and long-limbed giants, three metres tall or more. One looks scaly. Another is covered in thick fur.

They seem to be human, but like the creatures I've seen outside in the zones of the Mid Deck, they've mutated. And they don't look friendly.

I turn to see a winged creature standing behind me. The shock of the deformed body, with its jutting breastbone and knot of shoulder muscles, hits me all over again. It cranes its head forward, and I see that it does have a human head.

His lips move. But with my ears still buzzing from the white noise, I can't make sense of the sounds he's making.

Then I see a ripple of movement. A man is emerging from the rectangular pool. He's powerfully built, with broad shoulders and a flat stomach. He pulls himself up onto the metal surround and I notice his paddle-like hands and feet, webbed skin stretched between splayed fingers and toes. And, as he walks closer, I stare at the ow of curious flaps of skin down either side of his neck.

I've seen him before, I realize. This is the figure I glimpsed deep in the ocean, or someone like him.

A gill-man.

He says something to the wing-man, then the two of them start to examine me. They take my backcan, search my flakcoat. Caliph chitters in protest, but they don't seem interested in him. No, it's me they're checking. They're feeling under my arms, down my back; checking between my fingers and behind my ears. One of them forces my mouth open and the pair of them look inside; then, using a small pocket-light, they peer into my eyes, up my nose . . .

'What are you looking for?' I ask, but they ignore me.

They're being rough. Poking and prodding. Treating me like some kind of critter. And all the while they're muttering to one another, like they're ticking items off a list.

'I'm human,' I say. 'I . . .'

But they don't want to hear. I'm tied up and shoved to the floor. I thrash about helplessly.

Suddenly the place is lit up again. Two flashes this time, as blinding as the one before.

This time, the babble grows agitated. Some of the mutants take cover; others scatter, running off into the shadows.

Then someone appears beside us. I've never seen anyone more powerfully built. His neck's thick and cabled. He's got a barrel-chest, fists like rocks, limbs like tree trunks. His skin is leathery and scaled.

He leans down and picks me up by the front of my flakcoat as though I was no heavier than a feather. He holds me up in front of him, glaring fiercely, his dark eyes narrowed and mouth hard. He turns and grunts something to the others, who nod vigorously, then he shoves me under one massive arm and carries me up to the top of a gantry, where he dumps me on the floor. Then he leaves.

And there's nothing I can do.

I roll over and peer down at the mutants below. I can smell their unwashed bodies. I crane my neck for a better look, and – hot swarf! – I wish I hadn't.

With their wings, their gills, their scales or thick glossy fur, each of them is weird and frightening.

And when one of them – a giant with leathery skin –
looks up and starts shouting and waving his fist, I shrink
back and turn away.

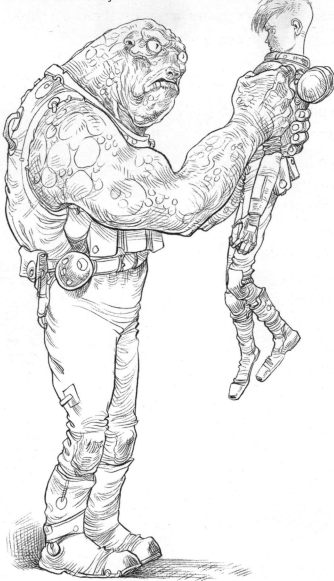

Just then, I feel movement inside my flakcoat. I look down and see Caliph emerging from my pocket. He scrambles up the front and his whiskers tickle my chin. I nuzzle my cheek against him as best I can, mumbling through the gag how glad I am to see him.

And I *am* glad.

But then he's off again, scampering along my arm. He sniffs at the cords binding my wrists and I feel a soft vibrating as he starts to gnaw through the leather. I keep my arms flexed and all at once, it snaps. Hands free at last. I realize my ears have cleared too. I can hear again.

'Good boy!' I whisper as I untie the cords at my ankles.

All at once, from high above our heads, there is a third blinding flash. It's bigger and brighter than the others – and it keeps on going.

15

The mutants are in disarray. Below me, they scatter in all directions.

Wing-men – dozens of them – have taken up positions at the tops of the tallest gantries. Scale-men and fur-men are hurrying across the floor of the chamber, darting from pillar to pillar towards different points close to the outer walls. A separate group is taking up position near the bottom of the chimney I came in through. They're all holding the white-noise weapons – small globes that glow in their hands.

Suddenly a panel in the wall of the chamber bursts open. A zoid steps through, its lasers blazing.

It's not like the maintenance zoids that Belle and I saw putting out the fire. No, this one is like some kind of simple humanoid. It's big, with two arms, two legs, a visored head and heavy body armour. If my recon-sight was working, I bet it would be showing the red heat-sig of a killer.

Behind it, buzzing like angry flies, are the small zoids with the lens-heads. They dart through the air as the lumbering zoid rakes the chamber with laser fire.

A fur-man falls to the ground, his chest smoking. A wing-man is shot from an upper

gantry, falls screeching through the air and lands with a sickening crunch.

The mutants respond with their weapons. The globes in their hands glow brightly and the chamber fills with white noise. I shield my ears as the small zoids start to spin out of control and crash to the floor. But the humanoid zoid doesn't seem to be affected. It strides across the chamber on armoured legs, and begins to climb the ladder towards the gantry I'm crouching on.

Just then a mutant drops down onto the gantry from above and lands beside me. He's thin and wiry, with scaled skin. Black, unblinking eyes fix themselves on mine.

They're filled with hate and rage, like he's blaming me for the attack. The zoid appears behind him. Its arm jerks and thrums, and a beam of laser light shoots from it. It hisses through the air and slams into the scale-man's back. He looks puzzled for a moment and looks down to see smoke exploding from his chest – then, arms and legs splayed, he falls heavily on his front. Dead.

The zoid comes closer and I can see just how big it is. Two metres tall, at least.

I scuttle backwards, my arms raised to protect myself.

The zoid doesn't shoot. Instead it extends an arm towards me.

Resistance is futile. There's nothing I can do.

The zoid's hand closes around my arm in a vice-like lock. It pulls me down the ladder and back across the smoke-filled chamber. The white noise dies away as the mutants cease firing.

They're letting us go.

The zoid steps through the hole it blasted in the chamber wall and drags me after it. Only as I enter the darkness do I realize that something is missing. There is no small warm body curled up inside my flakcoat.

I have left Caliph behind.

16

The zoid heads swiftly down a dark tunnel – some sort of
air duct or ventilation shaft. It's taking me with it. Behind
us, the surviving flying zoids hover and buzz, their lens-
heads swivelling in constant surveillance.

Far ahead, I see a light. We keep on towards it.

The zoid is moving slowly and steadily now, lurching
from side to side as it continues up the sloping tunnel.
By the time we arrive at the entrance, I'm feeling queasy
with motion-sickness. And it doesn't get any better when
we step outside. It's stifling hot here. The air's heavy and
humid and sickly sweet.

We're in some kind of swamp zone.

The grow-troughs here are long and narrow, and
laid out in lines that stretch far into the distance. They
contain mud that is as brown and thin as soup. Tangles
of fat-leafed bushes with stilt-like roots are growing out
of it.

A sharp-toothed creature with angular green scales
appears from the shadows and lurches towards us.
But the zoid zaps its laser at it, and it spins round and

splashes away. Somewhere close by, a pair of birds are screeching at one another.

And there are insects. Thousands . . . millions of insects, hovering over this wetland, buzzing and humming. They're attacking one another, or dive-bombing the grow-troughs for food – until they realize there's something even better to feast on.

Me.

Suddenly they're all over me. I can feel them. In my hair, on my face, crawling into my ears and up my nose. I spit and wriggle, but it's hopeless. There's nothing I can do to keep them from biting me, stinging me; eating me alive.

One of the flying zoids approaches. The clear lens at the front of its head is pointing directly at me. The iris focuses.

All at once a section at the top of the zoid's tubular body slides back and a nozzle appears. I feel a damp spray on my skin and close my eyes. The spray is cool and soothing, and the stinging of the insect bites disappears. I open my eyes to see that the insects have all retreated. They're still there, but keeping their distance. It's as though I'm in some kind of force-field that's keeping them at bay.

We continue through the swamp.

Our progress has slowed right down. The zoid's legs

have extended and it's plodding
through the grow-troughs, testing
the firmness of the bottom with
each step before putting its weight
down. The mud gloops and gurgles. Bubbles of
gas rise up from the depths and pop at the
surface, filling the air with that sickly
sweet odour I first smelled when we
emerged from the tunnel.

'Where are you taking
me?' I ask.

But the zoid doesn't answer. I'm not even sure it can.

We come to some kind of a walkway. It's raised up on
a criss-cross framework and jutting out over the rows of
grow-troughs. The end is jagged and splintered. Once,

it extended from one side of the swamp zone to the other. But some time in the past, something must have smashed into it, causing half of it to break off and sink into the muddy troughs below.

The robot grips the two side-rails and, using its hydraulic arms and legs, pulls us up onto the walkway. Then it does something that *really* surprises me. Leaning forward, it lowers me till my feet touch the surface of the walkway, and releases its grip.

I rub life back into my arm. Gradually feeling returns to my numb, tingly limbs.

The zoid motions for me to walk ahead. It prods me with the laser, which is pointed squarely at my back.

Suddenly the zilched walkway starts moving under my feet and we're speeding over the swamp. The insects come with us. But then, abruptly, the swamp is behind us, and they're gone. We're in a dry flat landscape now, fine dust and huge balls of tangleweed blowing in and out of the derelict buildings we speed past.

Several minutes later, the walkway comes to an end and we step onto the next one. And we're off again.

We're passing through a scarred landscape of broken tower-blocks and twisted masts set in bleached gravel, and rows of warehouse units, their visiglass windows smashed and rusted walls collapsing. Everything's in drab shades of brown and grey. The arc-lights are full on and the air above the parched earth shimmers with heat.

It looks like liquid. But there's no water here. Nothing grows. There's no birdcall, no critter-cry.

This whole area must once have been living quarters, home to the bio-engineers and their families. But now it is an abandoned place.

A dead place.

Up ahead, I see something gleaming. It's small and rounded at the top, and looks as though it's floating on an ocean.

As we come closer, the

mirage melts away, and I see a dome set in the middle of a broad, raised slab of polished stone. It looks clean and cared for; so different from the derelict buildings we just passed. And it's vast too, some seventy metres high and ten times that in width. It's made of hexagonal pieces of visiglass, the individual panes set in an intricate framework of urilium struts. The light reflecting off the visiglass makes it impossible to see inside. As the walkway brings us nearer, I notice the series of entrances at the base of the dome.

The walkway comes to an end. We step onto the grey slab and climb a flight of broad stairs set into the stone. At the top, a circular door opens. I hesitate. The zoid shoves me forward, into the glowing white airlock, then follows me inside.

'Decontamination sequence activated,' says a voice.

17

It's cool inside. In front of me is a second door, thick and heavy-looking. A visiglass tube appears from the ceiling above and lowers itself over me.

I feel claustrophobic. My heart thumps.

The visiglass begins to glow a deep red, and on its surface a display of moving holographic lines and circles appear. They flit and flicker in ever-shifting patterns. There's a buzzing noise, and the tube is criss-crossed with laser light. It cuts through my clothes, which fall to the floor in a powder of ash.

Suddenly the red light turns green. The visiglass tube rises and disappears back inside the ceiling.

There's a *clunk* and a *hiss*, and small holes in the side walls emit a fine spray. I'm surrounded by mist. Apart from the smell, which is sour and antiseptic, it's just like a vapour shower. Then the spray stops and the airlock is filled with warm jets of air.

'Decontamination completed,' says the voice. 'Prepare for genetic validation.'

Behind me, I'm aware of movement, and when I turn, I

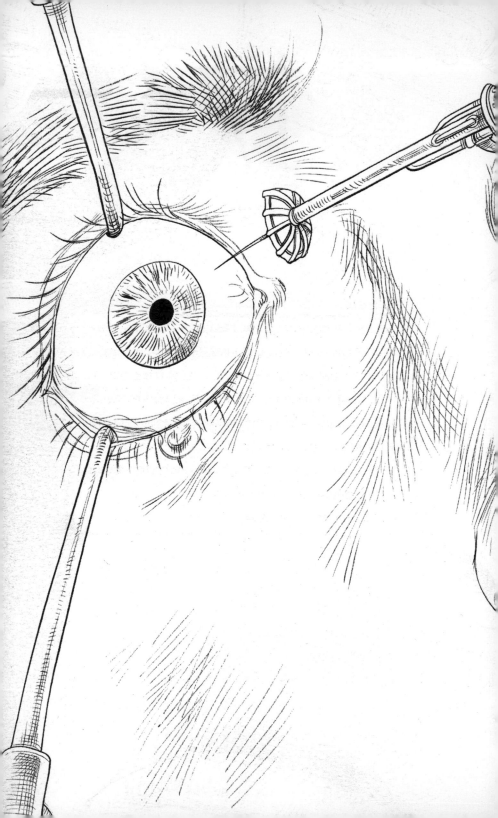

see the zoid. It does not speak. As I watch, a long black nozzle extends from its hand. It comes closer. I try to push it away, but it's hopeless. The zoid reaches out with the other hand and pins my head against the wall.

Its metal fingers prise my eyelids apart. The nozzle whines and pulsates as it approaches my eyeball. I want to scream, but no sound comes out. The end of the nozzle presses against my eye . . .

And everything goes black.

I don't know how long I've been out for, but when I come round, everything's changed.

I'm lying on a table in the middle of a white room. I'm dressed in a white tunic and trousers, and soft polysynth boots.

The zoid is standing over by a metal worktop. The silver surface is covered with surgical instruments, gleaming tools. I don't know what they are, or what they're for. But I don't like the look of them.

The zoid turns to me. 'You are awake,' it says. So it can speak.

I swallow. I can hardly deny it.

It looks at a stream of holo-data hovering in the air above my head.

'You have passed genetic validation, and you appear calm and lucid,' it tells me. 'Negligible threat levels. Good. We can now get acquainted properly.'

The zoid walks towards me and looks down. I see myself mirrored in the shiny visor. Then it reaches up, presses side-panels and removes the zoid helmet. Next thing I know, there's a *click* and the chest armour opens.

And a human climbs out.

He doesn't look that much older than me. He's pale and freckled, with cropped black hair. His nose is broad, his ears are small and he's got blue eyes that are staring at me like I'm some kind of freak.

'Greetwell,' he says. 'I'm Travis.' And he sticks out a hand.

I get up off the table and shake his hand. I'm shocked by how soft it is. This is the hand of someone who's never done a day's physical work in his life.

'York,' I tell him. I want to ask him what this place is and why he's brought me here, but he's in no mood to talk.

'Come with me, York,' he says.

We cross the room to a door on the far side. It slides open with a soft *swoosh*, and we step through.

'Hot swarf!' I gasp.

I'm standing in a towering atrium. Ancient trees grow from floor to ceiling, and there are hanging troughs, packed with flowers and trailing plants, attached to cables so fine it looks as though they're suspended in mid-air at every level.

Beyond the atrium is a wall of brightly lit-up visiglass. It's some fifteen storeys high and stretches off in both directions as far as I can see. Elevators are attached to

95

its front, travelling both up and down and side to side. Each storey has a visiglass ceiling and floor, and is sub-divided into what seem like countless individual rooms by visiglass walls.

And it's weird. Through these visiglass ceilings and floors and walls, I can see what each one contains. The inner workings. It's almost like my recon-sight's working again. There are comp-stations, info-decks, power-units, holo-banks, sleep-pods, trough-gardens, rec-halls, screen-rooms, medi-cabins . . .

And a whole lot of people.

Not mutants, but humans like Travis. Like me. Hundreds, definitely; maybe thousands. They're at every level of the massive dome, occupying every space; working, resting, playing.

Travis turns back to me. 'There'll be time to look round later,' he says and, taking me by the arm, he leads me through the atrium garden, where a work-gang of gardeners are weeding the flower beds and trimming the shrubs.

We come to one of the elevator points. Travis presses his hand to a circular pad moulded into the visiglass. I look up to see an elevator speeding down to us. It slows as it approaches, then glides to a stop. The door slides open, and we step inside.

'Level fourteen,' he says, 'twenty-four, seventy, ten.'

A woman's soft voice repeats his destination.

'Affirmative,' says Travis. And we're off.

I've braced myself for going up, and when we suddenly speed to the left, it takes me by surprise and I stumble. Travis steadies me and I grab hold of the safety rail. Room after room blurs past. Then we stop again, and this time we do go up – and so fast, my stomach lurches and my knees bend. Beneath me, I can see the floor recede as we climb higher and higher, until I'm feeling so dizzy I have to look away.

Travis is grinning. 'Pretty impressive, eh?' he says.

I grin back. 'It's amazing,' I say, but am aware of the tremble in my voice.

Fourteen floors up, we come to a stop for a second time, but the elevator door doesn't open. Instead, we set off, horizontal again, this time heading *inside* the stacked banks of rooms and chambers, down a long square tunnel.

We're travelling more slowly now. Other than a low hum, there's no noise in the elevator, but I catch glimpses of what's going on all around.

Swimmers in a pool below me. A bev-counter above, with men, women and children at tables or propping up the bar. Three men working at a silver machine that's dispensing some kind of pills to my right. Then a bank of sleep-pods; some of them occupied, some empty. A man at a comp-screen. A woman at a mirror, brushing her hair.

It's creeping me out being able to see everything like this. Back at my old home in the Inpost, I had places to hide away. To be on my own. To think about stuff. Here, everyone's on display.

Travis doesn't seem to even notice.

'There's no privacy here,' I say. 'Doesn't that bother you?'

'Bother me?' he says, one eyebrow raised. 'Why would it bother me? I've got nothing to hide.'

I let it go. Moments later, we come to a smooth halt.

'Twenty-four, seventy, ten,' the voice purrs.

The door opens and Travis

ushers me into the room beyond it. I look round, still wondering what I'm doing here.

From what I've seen so far, this is one of the larger chambers in the dome. Broad and deep, it extends upwards two storeys, the ceiling formed by the frame of the geodesic dome itself. Given its size, there's not much furniture in it. There's a large desk at the centre of the floor. Behind it is a chair, its high back towards me. A stool. An info-stack.

And all of them looking like they're floating in mid-air.

I don't think I'll ever get used to the see-through floors in this place. I'm dizzy. My stomach's clenched. I know the visiglass is thick and strong, but I can't help feeling I'm just about to plummet down through the air.

I grip the edge of the desk. Look down at my feet. Below them is a storeroom where men and women in blue tunics are unpacking large boxes. And below them, a workroom where a couple of techies are dismantling one of the flying zoids. And below them, a work-station where three women are staring at holo-screens. And below them . . .

I hear someone clear their throat and look up to see the high-backed chair in front of me has swivelled round. A woman is sitting in it. She's got thick silvery hair, tied up in three buns. She's wearing a high-necked white tunic and there's a thin tinted transparent band over her

eyes – which are blue and intense and staring, not at me, but at something she can see in the band.

Then they refocus. On me. She flashes me a smile that reveals a set of perfectly even white teeth. And I look back at her, feeling a little intimidated, this weird hot-cold tingly sensation shooting up and down my spine.

'You are York, I understand,' she says, and the voice is soft and friendly.

'I am,' I say.

'And you come from the Outer Hull.'

'I do.' I wonder how she knows.

She must have noticed my confusion. 'The surveillance droids spotted you soon after your arrival in the Mid Deck,' she says, then frowns. '*Two* of you. You weren't easy to track . . .'

'That . . . that was my friend. Belle,' I tell her. 'We got split up.'

She stares at me for a moment, then smiles again. 'I see,' she says, and she leans forward, her arms sliding across the top of the desk.

'Greetwell, York from the Outer Hull,' she says. 'And welcome to the Sanctuary. My name is Crockett – Petra Crockett – and I am going to ask you some questions. Please answer them as honestly as you can.' Her eyebrows twitch. 'I shall know if you're lying.'

The questions are easy at first. How old I am. What

happened to my parents. Whether I have any brothers
or sisters. But soon they probe deeper. How many live
in the Outer Hull? Where do they live? I answer as best
I can, and then she wants to know *why* they hide away,
and how long for, and how we survive – and then we
get onto the Rebellion, and killer zoids, and me being a
scavenger . . .

The woman is so open and friendly that the unease I
felt when I first met her is washed away. And it seems so
long since I've talked properly to another human being,
I find I want to tell her all about myself; to be accepted
into this new world of order and stability that I've
stumbled across.

'These parts that you scavenge, York,' she says, that
smile of hers flickering on her lips. 'You say that your
people modify themselves with them.'

I nod. 'If we get injured, yes. Zoid arms, legs . . .'

'Robotic mutants,' she says quietly.

She is no longer smiling, and I realize how lucky
it was that Belle was not brought here with me. She
glances at Travis, then back at me.

'It is fortunate for you, York,' Petra Crockett says,
her voice cold and clipped, 'that you have passed our
genetic validation.'

19

'The bev-counter,' Travis says, and gives the destination number to the elevator.

He seems friendlier now, and I guess it's cos I did OK answering Petra Crockett's questions. As the elevator darts its way through the maze of visiglass tunnels, he points out various places I might find of interest.

'That's one of our gyms,' he says, waving a hand towards a hall where twelve or so men and women are working out on machines. 'There's one on every level,' he adds. 'That's a recycling depot. Nothing goes to waste in the Sanctuary. And that,' he says a while later, 'is a crèche.'

I find myself looking into a large room filled with about a hundred young children, both toddlers and crawlers. They're all busy playing – with holo-bricks or info-pads; the more advanced of them scrambling over a climbing cube.

'Note the thick red mat on the floor,' Travis says, and I nod. I already had. 'It's cos little kids don't like being on a visiglass floor,' he explains. 'Freaks them

out, crawling over nothing.'

I know how they feel.

'They won't play anywhere else till they're five at least,' Travis goes on. 'Then they're fine with it.'

A couple more up-down-side-to-side twists and turns and the elevator announces that we've arrived at our destination. The bev-counter. The door slides open, and I'm immediately struck by a smell makes my stomach rumble.

We step inside.

The place is half full. There are people perched on tall stools at the counter or seated around small silver-topped tables. A couple of servers are working behind the counter, pouring mugs of froth-topped bev, or doling out bowlfuls of something green, which another couple of servers are loading onto trays and delivering to the tables.

The babble of conversation seems friendly enough. But as we walk through the diners it gets quiet, and people look up at me suspiciously. Some frown. Others look away.

'You're probably the first new face any of them have ever seen,' Travis tells me.

'Greetwell,' someone calls.

We turn, and I see someone fair-haired beckoning to us.

'We grew up together,' Travis tells me as we head towards him. 'Birth-pod, nursery, crèche, tech-school, security watch . . . York, this is Grant,' he says when we reach him. 'Grant, York.' He smiles. 'It's OK. York has been validated.'

Travis says this loudly so the others can all hear.

'So, Petra has accepted you,' says Grant, shaking my hand. We sit down at the table. 'Interesting.'

'The Sanctuary is scaled,' Travis tells me. 'We have a population of three thousand, and that remains constant. It's the number the Sanctuary can best sustain. Birthing takes place every three years, one hundred newborns each time, and we live to ninety.'

I frown. 'What, ninety exactly?'

The pair of them nod. 'We've got the tech here to make sure of that,' says Grant. 'No one dies before they're ninety.'

'And people who live to be *older* than ninety?' I ask.

Travis laughs. 'That's not encouraged,' he says – and I'm about to ask him what *that* means, when one of the servers arrives at our table. He's holding a tray loaded up with three mugs, three bowls and a small plate with twenty-one coloured pills on it. Travis thanks the server, then turns to me. 'Tuck in,' he says.

I sip the bev. It's sweet and salty at the same time, but refreshing. Then it's time to try the green stuff in the bowls. I take a spoon and cut a bit off, put it in my mouth and it tastes of . . . well, nothing. Nothing at all. It's just a kind of juicy, textured pap. I chew and chew, the stuff going from one cheek to the other as I try my best to swallow it – without success.

I look up to see that both Grant and Travis are staring at me. And when our eyes meet, the pair of them burst out laughing.

'What *is* it?' I mumble, mouth still full.

'Soylent,' says Grant. 'A mix of soya and lentils.'

'I'll show you the grow-troughs later,' says Travis. 'If you're interested,' he adds.

'And you eat this stuff?' I say, finally managing to swallow it down.

'You have to take the pills with it,' says Travis. 'For vitamins, minerals. And taste.'

He plucks seven of them from the plate, each one a different colour, then lays them out in a row. Grant leans across and switches two of them round, then the pair of them sit back.

'I recommend you eat them from left to right,' Travis says. 'And swill your mouth out with the bev between pills.'

And I do so.

The first pill is pale blue. I take another spoonful of the soylent, place it on the top, then start chewing – and this time my mouth is filled with a delicious fishy taste.

'Excellent,' I say.

I take a mouthful of bev, then try the next pill. It's brown. And meaty.

'Now, that's *really* nice,' I say.

And so it goes on down the line. The green one tastes of succulent vegetables. The yellow one gives the soylent a rich creamy flavour, the dark blue a hot, herby taste that makes my tongue tingle, and the red – well, that's really special. It's like every fruit I've ever eaten, all rolled into one. Finally, there's only one pill left. The white one. I place it on the last spoonful and stick it in my mouth. At first there's nothing, but then it explodes into flavours – sweet satzcoa and strong bev mixed together, and popping with spices that continue until I've swallowed every last bit.

'Enjoy?' says Travis, who has been watching me closely.

'Fantastic,' I tell him.

'Glad you like it,' he says. 'And it's just a fraction of the tastes on offer.'

'Yeah, you wait till you taste a *purple* pill!' says Grant. 'That really *is* fantastic.'

With the meal over, Travis takes me to my quarters.

'Level seven, thirty-one, thirty-one, thirteen,' the elevator purrs softly.

We step into a room that's bathed in red light, and with visiglass walls that anyone can see in through. I don't like it, but I'm so tired I try not to let it bother me.

There's a long padded bench in the middle of the room, storage space to the left, a vapour-shower to the right, and between them, jutting out from the far wall, a black sleep-pod.

A glowing panel on the headboard reads *Connor*.

Travis goes over to it, deletes the name and replaces it with *York*.

'You should sleep soundly, York,' he says. 'I've re-set the pod to your personal requirements.'

'What happened to Connor?' I ask.

Travis smiles. 'You have replaced him,' he says.

When I wake up, I feel wonderful. I've just had the best
night's sleep of my life.

I'm relaxed and clear-headed. My muscles seem
soothed, as though they've been massaged while I was
asleep. I roll over and the surface of the bed remoulds
itself to my new position. The temperature is perfect,
neither too hot nor too cold. I stretch and yawn, and the
pod emits a gentle, refreshing breeze.

I think of my mission. To discover what caused the
robot rebellion. I still haven't learned why I've been
brought to the Sanctuary. But maybe, just maybe, the
answer lies here.

It's what I need to find out . . .

I sit up. The lid of the pod opens up and I climb out.
All around me, the Sanctuary pulses with life. I gaze
through the visiglass walls at other sleep-pods, their
occupants emerging, looking as well-rested as me. And
it's odd. No one looks back. No one seems aware I'm
even there – which suits me just fine.

I guess it's how they must deal with the lack of privacy.

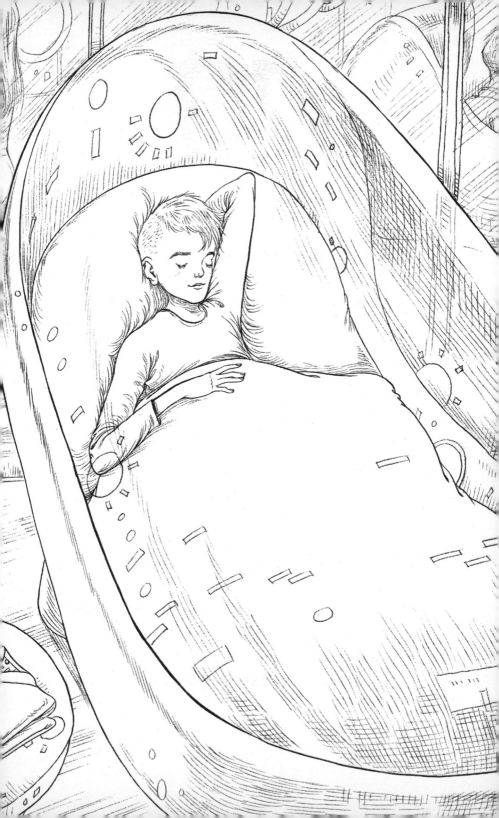

Crisp new clothes are lying on a heated pad beside the pod. I put them on. Four levels down, I see the bev-counter is beginning to fill up with the first of the day's diners. My stomach growls and I decide to join them, wondering what new tastes the pills have in store for me.

I walk to the door of my room and I'm trying to remember what the co-ordinates to the bev-counter are, when the elevator arrives. Its door swishes open and Travis is standing there.

'Saw you were up,' he says with a smile. 'Thought you might need some help finding your way around.'

'Thanks,' I say, and step into the elevator.

'Twenty-seven, twenty-three, eleven,' says Travis, and it takes us to the bev-counter.

Blue, yellow, red pills. Explosions of taste on my tongue. Citrus. Smoked meat. Then something sweet and creamy to finish off with. It's as delicious as my meal the night before, and Travis smiles back at me, pleased to see how much I've enjoyed it.

Around us the other diners are relaxed and welcoming. It's like they've accepted me. And that makes me feel so good. I sit back, warm, rested, well fed and happy.

Just like everybody else.

If only the whole of the Biosphere was like the Sanctuary, I find myself thinking. Perhaps it once was.

Back in the Launch Times. I remember the hologram of the bio-engineer with his ancient flight-suit and flawless white teeth out there in the zones . . .

And with a sudden pang I remember that Belle's out there too. And Caliph. Little Caliph, lost in the mutants' lair . . .

Travis breaks into my thoughts. His face looks serious.

'We are some of the last humans in the universe,' he tells me, his gaze flicking round the crowded bev-counter. 'We have to stick together.'

I nod. It's what we used to say up in the Outer Hull – though this ordered dome of comfort and safety seems a world away from that.

'The Sanctuary protects us, and we have to protect it . . .'

'From zoids?' I ask.

Travis shakes his head. 'There are no zoids here, York,' he says. 'The force-field kept the Outer Hull rebellion from the Mid Deck. Our robots and droids are just that: robots and droids. Uncontaminated. Serving humans.' He scowls. 'But the same cannot be said of the Outsiders.'

'You mean the mutants?' I ask. 'Are they human?'

'No, York. They are *not* human,' Travis tells me firmly. 'Don't ever, *ever* make that mistake. They've been contaminated, and there's nothing they'd like better than

to contaminate us.' His voice trembles with emotion. 'Which is why we have to keep them out.'

He fixes me with that intense unblinking stare of his, as if weighing me up.

'I don't know how much you lot up in the Outer Hull know about the history of the Biosphere,' he says.

'I know the Earth was dying,' I tell him, recalling the info I was fed by the Half-Lifes back at the Inpost. 'And that humans used the last of its resources to build the Biosphere, to store everything that was good and useful and should not be lost.'

Travis is nodding.

'I know that a thousand years ago, we set out across the vastness of space in search of a new Earth,' I go on. 'With tech-engineers, bio-engineers, core-controllers. And robots. And that five hundred years after that, something malfunctioned at the Inner Core. The robots rebelled against the tech-engineers in the Outer Hull . . .'

'Precisely,' Travis breaks in. 'So here in the Mid Deck, our bio-engineers triggered the safety protocol. Above and below, the Mid Deck sealed itself off from any contamination.'

His eyes narrow thoughtfully. It's as if he's reliving that moment – a moment that took place hundreds of years before he was even born.

'But we had another enemy,' he tells me. 'An enemy

within. Accelerated evolution. It started in the labs, spread to the archives and seed banks. And then out into the zones. We lost control of them one by one. Life evolved, mutated, and the zones broke down, merged, became one huge messed-up zone. A chaos zone.' He passes a hand slowly over his cropped black hair. 'Some blamed the zoids of the Outer Hull for cutting power-lines; some blamed the controllers at the Inner Core for the failure of central filtration systems. But whatever caused accelerated evolution, there was only one solution. Retreat to the Sanctuary and decontamination.

'Three thousand of us there were then. Three thousand there are now. No more. No less. To allow any others into the Sanctuary would ruin what we have here. It's what the Outsiders can't understand. And what they can't understand,' Travis says, shaking his head, 'they seek to destroy.'

21

'But come, York,' Travis says, and claps his hands together. 'If you've had enough to eat and drink, I thought I'd take you to see our other new arrivals.'

I look up. 'There are others?' I say, surprised.

And he smiles. 'You'll see.'

I follow him back to the elevator and soon we're gliding through the Sanctuary. It occurs to me that I'm not really noticing the individual hustle and bustle of the dome any more, just the atmosphere as a whole.

It's calm. Well ordered. Harmonious . . .

I smile sadly to myself. I'm getting used to being a part of this peaceful community, and I only wish that Belle and Caliph were here to share it with me. The thing is, though, I know now that neither of them would have been allowed in.

There are no zoids or critters in the Sanctuary.

The elevator comes to a stop. The door slides open and we step into a softly lit room with soothing music playing. It's full of young men and women, each of them cradling an infant in their arms. Wrapped in white shawls, the babies are gazing up into their parents' adoring faces and gurgling happily.

I don't remember my own parents. They were killed by the zoids when I was a baby back in the Outer Hull. My eyes mist over. How lucky to be born here in the Sanctuary, safe in the knowledge that you'll live a long and happy life.

What was it Travis said? Ninety years?

Just then, from behind me, the elevator opens once more and a group of grey-haired people troop out into the room. They mingle with the young parents and their newborns, marvelling at the babies' tiny fingers and toes, and cooing over them lovingly. I look at them them. Parents and grandparents sharing the joy of new life . . .

Then, as Travis and I stand there, the parents take their babies off in elevators to crèches in other parts of the Sanctuary. The grey-haired people watch them go.

The music fades. The lights brighten.

I notice that Petra Crockett is looking down at us from her chamber high up in the dome. She nods, and Travis nods back at her. It's only then that I see that droids have arrived.

They're tall and thin, with black bodies and visored faces. They escort the old people into a waiting elevator. The door closes and the elevator drops down into the depths of the Sanctuary, its lights dimming before it disappears from view, like an energy pulse down a generator well.

When it returns, moments later, the elevator is empty.

'Where did those people go?' I ask Travis, though I'm not sure I want to hear the answer.

'The Sanctuary sustains us, York,' Travis says. 'And we, in our turn, sustain the Sanctuary. Three thousand. No more, no less. The elders have greeted the newborns and have departed. The Sanctuary continues.'

He takes me by the arm and guides me towards the elevator.

'Now come and see what we do for recreation,' he says with an easy laugh. 'As a scavenger you should enjoy this.'

But what I have just seen has shocked me. The Sanctuary is a wonderful haven. In the Outer Hull a scavenger like me is lucky to reach thirty years. Almost nobody up there survives long enough for their hair to go grey, let alone live till they're ninety.

And yet . . .

'The Sanctuary took me in,' I say slowly. 'Does that mean Connor . . . ?'

'Connor is no longer with us,' Travis says simply, and turns away.

The elevator brings us to a broad visiglass platform. A holo-screen hovers over us, and a group of young people are sitting on synth-foam cushions with consoles in their hands. Everyone is having a good time, laughing and joking around.

Two boys of about eleven or twelve are squaring up to each other playfully.

'Going to have a good one, Lennox?'

'I'm gonna be unstoppable, Klute. Full power!'

As I watch, they turn their attention to the holo-screen. An image comes into focus.

It's an arena of some sort, an expanse of sand enclosed by metal walls. The quality of the simulation is awesome. High-def graphics. Gigapixel res. I can't wait for the game itself to get started.

A siren sounds.

Klute and Lennox raise their consoles and settle themselves on their cushions ready for the contest. Their friends hush up. Everyone concentrates on the game.

Travis pulls up a couple of cushions and we join the spectators.

Up on the screen, there's a mutant. A gill-man. And I can't help it. A wave of revulsion comes over me. He's dressed in patched-up trousers. Overhead, two lens-head droids – one silver, one white – are doing a strange dipping, darting dance in mid-air. Around me, the audience whoop and cheer at the two gameplayers who, I now see, are operating the lens-heads with their consoles.

Lennox has the silver droid; Klute the white. They're hovering a couple of metres above the gill-man.

His eyes look round wildly. His teeth are bared. Having seen a gill-man up close, I can appreciate just how realistic the vid-designers have made him look.

'Let the game begin,' says a calm female voice, the words glowing briefly on the holo-screen.

The gill-man stumbles forward. He gathers himself, the skin-flaps at his neck trembling, then looks up at the two lens-heads hovering above him. Their apertures open and close as, beside me, Klute and Lennox's fingers play over the consoles.

'Careful,' someone in the crowd murmurs.

'He looks tough, this one,' says someone else.

All at once, the gill-man spins round and throws himself up at the silver droid, one webbed hand outstretched. He's fast, but not fast enough. His hand closes on nothing and he falls back down to the sandy ground.

And the two droids attack. Klute and Lennox's fingers are a blur.

The silver droid nudges in front of the white one. There's a flash, and a thin streak of blue taser-light shoots out from its head. It hits the gill-man square in the back. He folds double and slams to the ground, where he twitches and writhes, life-like drool spilling from the corners of his mouth.

The vid-designers really have excelled themselves. For a simulation, it's horribly real.

The spectators roar with delight and, down at the left-hand corner of the screen, a skull appears. Its eye-sockets glow a pale yellow.

Lennox looks across at Klute, a smile of triumph playing on his lips.

Klute scowls. 'It's not over yet,' he says.

The gill-man's picked himself up. He's stooping forward, arms out at his side, watchful, snarling.

Suddenly the white lens-head soars up into the air, turns in a tight arc, then dive-bombs him. The taser-light flashes blue. It strikes the top of his head. He reaches up protectively. The taser-light flashes again and again, making his body jerk and jolt, and forcing him backwards.

He's screaming, but silently, since the simulation is playing soft, playful music. There's smoke coiling up from his skin, his clothes. He stumbles, crashes to the ground.

And a second skull appears, in the right-hand corner of the screen this time. Its eye-sockets glow a deep amber.

'Yes,' Klute mutters grimly.

Lennox ignores him. He's bringing his own lens-head down low towards the gill-man, firing at his feet.

He may be a mutant, but I don't feel easy watching him being tortured like this. Unlike the crowd. They're loving it.

The taser-light stabs around the gill-man again and again, like a bird pecking at grain. Small black marks appear in the sand. Klute's white lens-head joins in.

The spectators are laughing – and when the taser-light actually scores a hit on the gill-man, they whoop with joy.

I look over at Travis, who's smiling broadly. He's clearly enjoying himself as much as the others.

The gill-man's on his feet now. Running. But there's nowhere to run to. Nowhere to hide. Both lens-heads are after him, taunting him, shooting at his feet. Sometimes

the taser-light hits him, sometimes it misses. Either way, as the blue light flashes – on-off, on-off – he keeps on leaping and jumping and skipping about, that same silent cry of distress on his face.

It's hard to watch.

Then he's down again. The air around me explodes with cheering. Everyone's looking at the two skulls in the corners of the screen expectantly – and suddenly the eye-sockets of Lennox's one turn a deep shade of orange.

Lennox smirks. Then, while Klute's bringing his white

lens-head around in the air, he puts his own silver lens-head into a dive. The spectators sense victory.

'Go! Go! Go! Go!' they're chanting.

With a yelp of triumph, Lennox stabs at his console. A stream of intense blue-white taser light hits the mutant full in the chest. He falls down. And this time he stays down.

The roar that goes up around me is deafening. The spectators are on their feet, jumping up and down with excitement, chanting Lennox's name. Klute's still firing at the gill-man.

But it's all over. The eye-sockets of Lennox's skull are pulsing a deep blood red.

'Arena decontaminated,' says the voice.

I swallow uneasily. I feel Travis's arm around my shoulder. 'What do you think?' he says.

I shrug. 'It . . . it seemed so real,' I tell him, and I can feel a painful lump in the back of my throat. 'That mutant character . . . He looked as though he was really suffering.'

And Travis laughs. 'Lighten up, York,' he says. 'It's only a game.'

23

We're back in the chamber up on the fourteenth level.
It's just the same as it was before – large and bright, with
the desk, the info-stack, the stool and the high-backed
chair. Except now the place is empty.

'Where's Petra?' I ask.

Travis looks round and shrugs. 'She'll be with us
shortly,' he says, then adds, 'Fancy a look-see from the
viewing platform while we're waiting?'

I agree of course. Everything about the Sanctuary
fascinates me.

We step towards the desk, then stop at the centre of
a circular line cut into the visiglass floor. Travis reaches
out and presses a couple of buttons on the control panel
on the armrest of the chair.

There's a *click* and a *hum*, and the circle turns
out to be a round panel set in the floor, which starts
to go up. We quickly rise to the fifteenth level and
beyond. Then, when our heads are about to touch the
curved top of the Sanctuary, the platform comes to a
smooth stop. I look out through the visiglass hexagons

that make up the geodesic dome.

'Quite a view, eh?' says Travis, his arm sweeping round in a broad arc.

He's not joking. It's spectacular.

I can see different bio-zones laid out in wedge-shaped segments. Some of them I recognize. There are the tops of the towering trees in the rainforest of Zone 3, where Belle and I first arrived in the Mid Deck. And there, a stretch of grassland; an expanse of desert – and the polar ice-field of Zone 4. Far to one side, I can just make out the gleaming ripples of the frozen waterfall, where the water cascaded out through the crack in the ocean zone.

It was fairly obvious down on the ground that the barriers between the zones had broken down, but up here the true chaos is clear to see. It's all gone to gunk. Sand dunes drift into pools and forests, vines and creepers snake out across the snow, and bio-zone specimens released from their habitats now roam free.

And it's all so vast. The Mid Deck stretches off as far as I can see. In comparison, the Sanctuary – large as it feels from the inside – is little more than a pimple in this sprawling landscape.

It's not surprising the occupants of the Sanctuary feel under siege. Back at the Launch Times, the bio-engineers laid out the zones perfectly. Now, they're all messed up, and we're surrounded by one huge zone.

This chaos zone. Full of mutations.

What had Travis called it? Accelerated evolution.

I picture the face of the gill-man in the holo-
simulation. The skin-flaps at the neck. The webbed
fingers and toes. And I feel a familiar shudder of
revulsion. That was just a simulation, but out there in the
chaos zone are mutants just like that, lurking in the dark
corners, waiting for their chance to break into this bright,
safe, visiglass world, bringing chaos with them.

And I hate them for it.

'Enjoying the view?' comes a voice from below us.

I look down to see Petra Crockett, one hand raised
to shield her eyes from the light, staring up at us. She's
smiling.

'Thought I'd show York the sights,' Travis calls down.

'Very good,' says Petra Crockett, 'but there's
something *I* want to show him too. Down here.'

And she must have activated the platform herself,
because all at once, we're going down. As we descend,
I see that the chamber has been transformed. All around
us now are walls of light, made up of huge flickering
panels.

Holo-screens. Dozens of them.

The platform slots smoothly back into place in
the visiglass floor, and Petra Crockett is there to

greet me. She's beaming happily.

'I'm so glad you're settling into the Sanctuary,' she says, then turns towards the holo-screens. 'Travis has shown you one view of the bio-zones. But here, York, is another, more detailed view.' She raises a hand towards the nearest screen. 'Temperate forest, for instance, with its mix of deciduous and coniferous trees.'

In front of me is a close-up of a tree that I recognize from the atrium of the viewing deck up in the Outer Hull. It's a common oak, with rough bark, broad branches and a dense covering of rounded leaves.

As I watch, the picture focuses on a cluster of acorns, and a small critter that, apart from its long bushy black-and-white tail, looks like Caliph – and again I feel a pang of loss. It's crouched on a branch, plucking them one by one and nibbling at them hungrily.

Petra moves to another screen, and there's another scene playing itself out. A snake-like creature is flying through mid-air, its body rippling from side to side, before wrapping itself round a dangling vine – and gulping down the squat, wide-mouthed critter that's crouched there . . .

'These images are from our maintenance droids,' she tells me. 'They're our eyes and ears. They help us know our enemy. Of course, we would like to venture out into the bio-zones more often ourselves, but . . .' She sighs. 'It is too dangerous for us, York. So we use the droids to monitor the extent of contamination. And the activities of the Outsiders.'

My attention turns to another holo-screen. Unlike the others, this one is a blur of static. Petra Crockett catches me looking at it.

'Another droid lost to their sonic weapons,' she says sadly. 'They are clever,' she concedes, 'the Outsiders. And they will stop at nothing to destroy what we have preserved here. Which is why we have to stop them . . .' Her eyebrows arch. 'Will you help us to do that, York?'

I feel a surge of anger towards the mutants. And it's strong. So strong I can't understand it. Or resist it.

'Yes,' I say. 'Yes, I will.'

24

'This is it,' says Travis.

Up in her chamber, Petra Crockett gave me a mission.
A dangerous mission. She asked me to go out into the
chaos zone and find one of her surveillance droids.

'A scavenger like you,' she said. 'I thought you might
enjoy the task.'

And of course she's right. Scavenging's what I do.

The droid went down somewhere near the
central library, and she seemed mightily
concerned about it. Apparently, it's vital
for the safety of the Sanctuary that the
information the droid collected is retrieved
by someone.

And that someone turns out to be me.

The elevator door opens, and I follow
Travis into the armoury. It's smaller
than I thought it would be, but
packed full of equipment.

Visiglass shelves line
the wall on one side

of the room. They're laden with boxes, each one with a glowing neon label on the front panel detailing its contents.

On the other side of the room are two rows of bulky exo-skeleton suits. I recognize them as the type Travis was wearing when he rescued me from the mutants. The arms and legs are ribbed with urilium rods, the chest reinforced with blast-proof shield panels, and the helmet visored. The whole thing is sealed and pressurized from within to prevent contamination.

I look critically at the huge, ungainly suits.

'I can't wear one of these,' I tell Travis. 'When I scavenge, I need to be able to see clearly and move about freely.'

Travis nods uncertainly. I can tell from his face he thinks I'm crazy. But he smiles and says, 'Tell me what you need.'

'Just basic kit,' I tell him. 'Like I had when I got here. Knee and elbow guards. A flakcoat. Boltdriver, a cutter . . .'

Travis walks past the row of suits and activates a compartment in the far wall. It slides open to reveal flakcoats and mech-tools. They look unused. I stare at a flakcoat in front of me. It's all but identical to my old one – the one I was wearing when I entered the decontamination chamber. If I hadn't seen it crumble to ash with my own eyes, I'd have sworn this was the same one.

'Try it on,' says Travis. 'See if it fits.'

It does. Perfectly.

It's a good sign. I feel my confidence rise. The mech-tools are good too – the cutter sharp and well weighted, the boltdriver handy and easy to use. I snap them into place. Over at the visiglass shelves, Travis pulls out box after box, and I arm myself with canisters of gunkballs, clips of grenbolts and a pulser. I load up the flakcoat. But not too much. I need to be light on my feet to scavenge.

When I'm done, I turn to Travis. It feels good being kitted out once more.

'Are you sure about this?' he says. He's looking me up and down, and seems worried.

'I think so . . .' I hesitate. 'Why? Is there something wrong?'

'It's just . . .' He frowns. 'York, I'm not sure you understand the implications of leaving the Sanctuary without wearing a safe-suit.' He nods over at the bulky exo-skeletons standing against the wall. 'Just one injury, York – the tiniest scratch – and you risk failing the decontamination protocol . . .'

'And then what?' I say. My heart's hammering inside my chest.

Travis can't hold my gaze. 'It won't just be your clothes that'll get incinerated,' he says quietly.

I swallow.

It occurs to me just how lucky I've already been. When I first came to the Sanctuary, it seems I was no more than one scratched hand away from incineration. But I have promised Petra Crockett that I'd scavenge her droid, and I can't back out now.

'Thanks for telling me,' I say to Travis.

If I pick up an injury, I won't be returning anyway. No, I'll go in search of Belle, I tell myself – although even as I do, I feel a strange sensation in the pit of my stomach. It is a clenched, knotted feeling, that gets stronger when I consider the possibility of not returning to this wonderful place.

It's as if the Sanctuary has some sort of invisible hold on me.

Travis claps me on the shoulder. 'But come, York. I'll take you back to your room. If you're going out there into the zones tomorrow, you'll need a good night's sleep.'

And despite everything, I do sleep well.

The sleep-pod really is amazing. The moment the lid

closes, the light dims and the pod adapts itself to the contours of my body, I fall into a deep sleep. And I don't wake again until eight hours later. When I open my eyes I feel rested, relaxed, but alert. Full of energy.

There's something else too. As the lid of the sleep-pod opens and I get up, I realize I'm no longer bothered at all by the visiglass walls around me. In fact I love the feeling they give me of being a part of the Sanctuary. I want to protect it more than ever, and when I think of it coming to harm I feel an intense anger, deep down inside me, just waiting to explode.

'Fully rested?' says Travis half an hour later, when I step out of the elevator down in the atrium beside the entrance.

And that's another thing. I now know the co-ordinates for the elevator to take me anywhere I want to go. It's really weird. They just pop into my head as if I'd learned them in my sleep.

I walk with Travis to the airlock. I'm dressed in my flakcoat, tooled up and ready to scavenge. Travis pats me on the shoulder and hands me a tiny ear-piece.

'Thank you, York,' he says. 'Petra asked you to wear this.'

I put it in my ear. It fits snugly, and I hear Petra Crockett's voice as the airlock opens and I step inside.

'No going back now,' it says. 'Good luck.'

I head down the stone steps, then stop. The swamp of Zone 2 lies ahead of me and I don't fancy crossing it again. Not with the swarms of biting, stinging insects buzzing over the scuzzy water.

'Take the walkway to your left, York,' comes a voice in my ear.

It's Petra Crockett again. Her voice is silky and smooth, yet it makes me jump.

'It will take you to the seed libraries. Zone 8. It is where we lost . . .' She hesitates. 'Where we lost the droid. Start your search there.'

'Will do,' I say.

'And York, this zone is unpredictable. More unpredictable than most, so keep moving. You have until nightfall to complete the mission and return.'

Her voice is as soothing as before, but I can hear a slight edge to it. Is it urgency? Impatience?

'I'll be as quick as I can,' I say.

'Excellent,' she purrs. 'Our databases are at your disposal. And there's a tracking device in your ear-piece. I'll do my best to guide you.'

I thank her and step onto the walkway to my left. It hums into motion, and I'm off, speeding through the Mid Deck.

As I leave the geodesic dome behind me, I find myself crossing a dry, barren plain. Zone 6. According to an info-post I pass, it used to be jungle. Not any more. There are dead trees, their branches like stubby fingers; there are clumps of dust-blown grass and long leafy tendrils that have grown out over the ground as far as they could, before the water gave out, stopping their growth and leaving them crisp and dried out.

The arc-lights overhead get hotter and hotter, simulating the temperature of the midday sun as I continue. I'm sweating inside my flakcoat. My eyes are screwed up against the dazzle.

I activate the coolant device.

The zones blur and change. Time moves on. Petra Crockett reminds me more than once of the urgency of my mission.

I come to signs of human habitation, all of them abandoned. A windowless tower, one side shored up by the fallen tree that smashed into it. A row of raised tanks that are rusted now and unable to hold water. A light-turbine, half of its black-and-white sails broken. And a series of tracks that criss-cross the entire zone.

'You are passing the magno-transport grid,' Petra tells me. 'Sadly non-functioning. But you might experience a little static interferen—'

Her voice is cut off by loud crackling.

Tracks cut through this dusty landscape like scars, and are marked by the shapes of stranded vehicles, their magnetic power units rusting beneath them. The static fades, and is followed by silence.

'You are approaching the central seed libraries.' Petra Crockett's voice is back, silky smooth. 'But time's moving on. I cannot impress upon you enough the importance of speed.'

The walkway slows, then comes to a stop. At last. I climb down onto a carpet of lush green grass.

I'm standing at the edge of a vast grassland. In the middle distance are terraces, connected by more walkways and full of stacks. They, like everything else, are covered in the grass, that is long and thick and ripples as the air from hanging turbines flows over it.

'Zone 8,' Petra Crockett confirms. 'The droid was downed on the upper levels of Bank 4.'

I set off, and find myself wading through the knee-high grass, its seed-laden heads swaying from side to side, puffing with pollen when I knock against them.

Having lived most my life in the Outer Hull, I found the other zones strange, but at least they were like places that once existed on Earth. This? This is weird. Truly weird. The grass is too thick. Too green. And it's like . . . I don't know. I'm probably being stupid, but it's as if I can hear it growing . . .

I haven't gone far when I stumble against something at my feet. I stop. Look down. And there's some kind of terminal there, lying on its side. The outer casing and screen are covered by a layer of grass.

And it's not the only one.

As I trudge deeper into the grassy zone, I'm surrounded by humps and mounds that form the outlines of consoles and work-desks, vid-screens and holo-stations. I'm wading through a vast bio-engineering hub, but one that's been completely overgrown with the thick, swaying grass.

'Keep moving.' Petra Crockett's voice is that same mixture of concern and irritation. 'If you slow down, the grass will seed itself.'

I look down and am shocked to see tiny grass shoots spotting the front of my flakcoat, the surface of my boots. Hot swarf! Something here is definitely not right.

'Ahead is Bank 4. Take the central walkway. Unfortunately it stopped working five centuries ago.'

'I can see it,' I tell Petra as a series of terraces comes into view up ahead. Like everything else, they're covered in the thick carpet of grass. 'I'm heading for it now.'

I climb the walkway, past terraces full of data-stacks that are shimmering and green-fringed. I reach the upper terrace and stop. There, stooped and unmoving, is the unmistakable outline of an exo-skeleton suit. It is covered with grass. I make my way over to it, and as I do, the ear-piece fills with static once more.

I'm on my own.

I take out my cutter and scrape away the grass covering the visored helmet. Etched beneath it is a name plate. *Connor*, it reads. I press the pressure-pads, the visor opens – and I'm staring into the dead eyes of the former occupant of my sleep-pod.

I swallow. It's no wonder Petra and Travis kept quiet about what happened to him.

With shaky hands, I shut the visor and step back, only to stumble over an object directly behind me. I crouch down and cut the grass away. It is the surveillance droid. The grass has seeded itself to its body and taken root in

the creases of metal. I can't believe how quickly the stuff grows.

I roll the droid over on its side. Then I unhook my boltdriver. It feels so good having it in my hand. Just like the old days back in the Outer Hull, doing what I do best.

Scavenging.

I cut through the lens casing and lay it to one side. The memory-unit is laid bare. I drill a hole in the urilium casing, and probe inside for the ejector-button. A moment later, there's a *click*, and the whole unit comes away in my hand.

'Memory-unit intact,' I whisper to myself. I put it in the pocket of my flakcoat. 'And secured.'

I leave the terraces and set off for the walkway, following the line of trampled grass, heading back the way I came. I'm feeling good. Happy to have been of use to the Sanctuary. Pleased that everything's gone without a hitch. And oddly elated to be out scavenging once again. I'm wondering whether Petra Crockett might not have other jobs like this for me when the lights abruptly go out.

'Nightfall,' the voice says in my ear. Petra Crockett is back again, and she doesn't sound happy. 'Have you secured the droid's memory-unit, York?'

I tell her I have.

'Then get out of Zone 8 as fast as you can,' she says.
Above me, the solitary arc-light shines down,
turning the swaying grass into a rippling sea of silver. I

increase my pace, only to see a long snaking trail of bio-luminescence coming towards me. It's between me and the walkway and, as I run, it swoops round and encircles me in a glowing, pulsating ring.

A head, mounted on a thick sinuous neck, rises up out of the grass. I come to a skidding halt. It's got four yellow eyes, a jutting snout, the jaws slightly parted to reveal three glistening fangs inside, and a pair of forked tongues that flick in and out between them. It is no more than a metre in front of me and, when I glance back, I see the snake-like creature's coils undulating all around me in the grass.

It's massive. And it has me surrounded. I'm trapped. The decontamination protocol back at the Sanctuary means I can't risk being bitten. Or even scratched. The coils contract; the jaws open wide. It's life or death . . .

The creature strikes.

A fang snags the shoulder of my flakcoat, and I stab wildly at its head with my cutter. There's a *squelch*. A *hiss*. And thick dark liquid spurts from its throat. The creature recoils. I pull out my pulser and fire.

Once. Twice. Three times.

Molten grenbolts find their mark and the creature's head explodes. I jump over the smoking stump and run. Run like my life depends on it. I've got to get out of this terrible zone.

I plough through the dense grass as fast as I can towards the walkway. I haul myself up onto its surface, which hums into life. I glance behind me. The creature's rearing up once more, and I see there are three smaller glistening heads already forming at the top of its severed neck as it does so. I stare back in fascinated horror as the walkway speeds me to safety. And when I reach the end, I step down, still shaken up.

'Keep moving!'

Petra Crocketts's voice jolts me back to action. I look down and realize the grass is fusing my boots to the ground. I yank them free and begin to run.

By the time I get to the dome, I'm close to exhaustion. My body is covered in a fresh green growth, weighing me down and growing faster than I can tear it away. But I'm all right. No cuts. No scratches.

I collapse against the sensor-pad. The door opens, and I fall forward into the airlock. The chamber seals with a hiss, and a calm voice speaks.

'Prepare for decontamination.'

26

'Decontamination complete,' the voice announces after what seems to me like an eternity.

For a second time the clothes I'm wearing have been lasered to ash. The kit – cutter, pulser, grenbolts – has been stripped down, cleaned and reassembled by a droid attendant. They're laid out on a tray at my feet next to the little ear-piece, gleaming and clean, just like me.

All in one piece. Thank the Half-Lifes!

The droid passes me crisp new clothes and polysynth boots. It has the memory-unit in one of its pincers. It waits patiently while I dress, then opens the inner airlock and leaves without a word.

I step through the doorway into the dome. And as I do so, I'm overwhelmed with a sense of belonging, of being where I'm meant to be.

Of being home.

It's a feeling that's made stronger by what's facing me. A huge crowd of people. They surge forward, grinning and laughing, whooping and cheering and calling out my name.

'York! York! York! York!'

I realize I'm grinning back at them. And waving. It feels so, so good to be back inside the Sanctuary, away from the horror of the chaos zone, and surrounded by all these people who are obviously relieved and pleased to see me.

'Well done!' someone yells.

'Yeah, well done, York!' several other cries go up.

'That was mega!' comes a voice, young and excited, and I turn to see Lennox, along with Klute and twenty or so of the young spectators from up on the simulation platform.

They're cheering louder than anyone, and as I step forward, they gather round me, patting me on the back, punching me lightly on the arms and beaming with happiness. And their reaction is so warm and friendly and sincere, I realize that I am now truly one of them.

'Thank you, thank you,' I say. 'But I was only serving the Sanctuary.'

And Petra Crockett, I think. The person who's made all this possible . . .

'The bev-counter,' someone calls out.

'Yeah, let's celebrate,' comes a chorus of voices. 'Drinks all round.'

I'm clutching my kit, laid out on the tray.

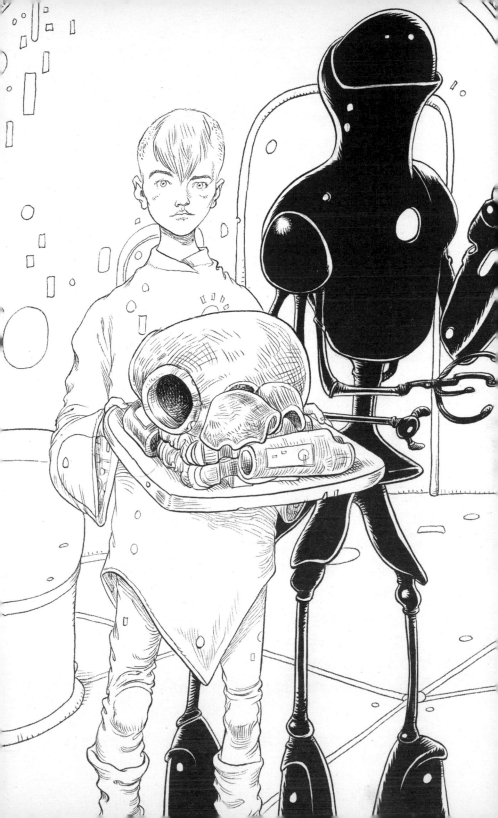

'That sounds great,' I say. 'But I need to get these things back to the armoury first. Then we'll celebrate!'

Another cheer goes up from the Sanctuary-dwellers, and the crowd parts to let me through. I step into a waiting elevator, give the co-ordinates, then wave back through the visiglass wall as it whisks me away.

As the crowd slips back into the distance, I look down at the tray and, I don't know why, but I pick up the ear-piece and pop it in my ear. Perhaps I want to see if it's still working. Perhaps I want to hear Petra Crockett's voice. Whatever the reason, I'm glad I do.

'After all, I rescued York.' It is the voice of Travis I hear. 'Why can't we rescue this companion of his?'

'It's too risky,' comes the reply. It's Petra Crockett.

So they know where Belle is now, I realize.

'But I'll be wearing a safe-suit,' Travis protests. 'And I'll insist that York does too. With twenty droids, we'll lose half, maybe more, but . . .'

'But nothing, Travis.' Petra Crockett is sounding exasperated. 'We rescued the boy because he was of use to us. Connor failed. York did not. The detonation droids did their job and destroyed the Outsiders' camp, but it was just an outpost, Travis. The girl is of no value.'

'But the Outsiders will torture her. Maybe kill her.' Travis sounds upset.

So am I. I swallow hard. Belle's out there in the

clutches of the hideous mutants. And Caliph. My little Caliph. I left him in the mutants' camp . . .

'Forget about rescue missions, Travis,' Petra Crockett insists. 'The memory-unit York recovered gives us the exact location of the mutants' central lair.'

'Beneath the hub-generator of Zone 12,' says Travis. 'York and I could go in through the duct tunnel . . .'

'Enough!' says Petra. 'This is the best chance we've ever had to destroy the mutants. Once and for all. Every last one of them. I won't let it slip through my fingers. And if the girl has to die that's no concern of mine.'

I've arrived at the armoury. The door opens, but I don't move. I can't stop listening.

'We send in the detonation droids,' Petra Crockett is saying. 'Every one we have—'

'The green light,' Travis suddenly interrupts her. 'The ear-piece is still active.'

'York?' I hear Petra Crockett. Her voice is suddenly smooth, calm and seductive. 'York, are you there?'

I hear Travis in the background.

'He's in the armoury . . .'

'York? How much have you heard?' There's a hard edge to Petra Crockett's voice now. 'Report to my chamber immediately. York? *York!*'

I remove the ear-piece and stand there for a moment. I don't like the sound of that voice. Or what it's been saying. I know where Belle is now and my plans have changed. I drop the ear-piece to the floor, and grind it to small pieces under my heel.

They won't be able to track me now.

I tool up. Fast, efficient, my mind racing. Then I stop and look at the rows of exo-skeleton suits. They stare back at me; big, bulky, protective. No one from the Sanctuary will go out into the zones without one on.

I smile.

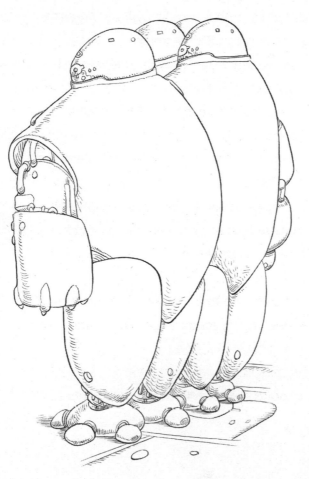

27

When I'm done, I hurry from the armoury. I give the elevator the co-ordinates, and it speeds back through the Sanctuary to the entrance. As I step out into the vast atrium, I look up through the visiglass levels.

High above, close to the top of the dome, I see Travis and Petra Crockett. They're coming down fast in an elevator of their own. My stomach lurches. I love their Sanctuary, but Belle comes first. Thing is, they must have triggered some sort of silent alarm, because more elevators, each one full of Sanctuary-dwellers, are coming towards me from all directions.

I activate the airlock door. It opens. I step inside. I'm in the decontamination chamber, staring at a spindle-legged droid, the lights on its head-unit lighting up as it receives its orders.

I don't give it a chance to act. Pulling my cutter from my belt, I kick away a leg, sending the droid clattering to the floor.

And I'm on it.

I plunge the point of the cutter down hard between

the riveted panels that separate the headpiece and body unit, then drag the blade to one side. A shower of white sparks explodes from the breached metal, followed by a jet of claggy zoid-juice. The air fills with the stench of molten circuitry.

I remove its data-chip and leap to my feet. I press the chip to the control panel of the outer door. It opens. I leave the Sanctuary. And run. And while I'm running, I reach into my flakcoat pocket and take out a fistful of small discs – the urilium seals that I removed from each and every one of the safe-suits in the armoury – and scatter them into the grow-troughs of the swamp zone.

Without the seals, the safe-suits are no longer safe. The Sanctuary-dwellers can't follow me now.

But their droids can.

I duck down behind a clump of marsh weed as I hear a tell-tale hum approach. The next moment, a lens-head comes flying past me, a beam of light from its eye scanning the swamp below.

It doesn't see me. I drop to my knees and begin to crawl.

Belle is out here at the mercy of the mutants, and whatever Petra Crockett thinks, I am not going to abandon her.

The droid is the first of many. The single arc-light shines down on the swamp, and the bushes, trees and matted tendrils are raked with the headlights of the flying lens-head droids as they continue their search.

I crawl on through the grow-troughs, mud and slime coating my hands and knees. It's dark and difficult to see which way I'm going, but at least the vicious insects are leaving me alone.

I'm looking for Zone 12 – the central hub-generator – and so follow the line of tall pylons that crosses the swamp. There are pylons just like these in the Outer Hull. They transport the power produced by the generators, and I'm hoping that these ones will lead me to the hub-generator where Belle's being held.

I'm in luck.

An info-stack tells me I'm in Zone 10. Almost there. I'm swiping away the holo-screen when the arc-lights come back on.

That's when I see them.

Large insects with bulbous bodies and ten thin articulated legs. There are hundreds of them, each one with a massive red eye at the centre of its head. They scuttle round me as I stand as still as I can.

Then, as I watch, they suddenly leap – in twos, threes, whole groups – high up into the air, and latch onto the power lines overhead. The cables fizz and spark. Then the insects let go and fall back down, their round bodies glowing for an instant, before they leap again.

They're feeding, I realize.

Trying not to disturb them, I pick my way carefully through this strange, rippling swarm. They're still all around me when the landscape changes again. I guess this must be the start of Zone 12.

It's a jumble of giant rusted containers, some overturned, others lying at strange angles, sand spilling from them. I scramble to the top of a tall sand dune and look back. The droids seem to be giving the bouncing energy feeders a wide berth, and I smile.

The curious insects have bought me some time.

I look ahead. Far in the distance, is a huge black-rimmed indentation in the sand, power cables converging and disappearing through an opening at its centre. It is ringed by circular covers – eight of them – all but one belching steam.

'Duct tunnels,' I mutter, remembering what I overheard through the ear-piece.

It takes me several hours to get to the hub-generator across the dunes. The location of the mutants' lair is making more and more sense to me. It's remote. The insects deter the droids. And even in my flakcoat and boots, I'm finding the going hard enough. Any Sanctuary-dweller in a safe-suit would find it next to impossible.

When I finally get to the generator I'm hot and tired, and my water flask is all but empty. I circle the rim of the hub and locate the one duct that isn't steaming. I drop to my knees and undo the grille that's covering it with my boltdriver, then pull it to one side.

I ease myself over the lip of the opening. Then, hands and feet braced against the two sides of the tubular duct, I lower myself into the darkness below. As I drop down, I start to hear distant noises, which get louder and louder the deeper I go. Voices, old and young.

The mutants in their lair far below.

At last, my feet touch the bottom. The duct tunnel is too low for me to stand upright. Head down and one hand outstretched before me, I hurry along it as fast as I can. I come to the end. Like the entrance to the duct at the top, it's covered with a metal grille.

I kneel and peer through.

The mutants' lair is vast, ten times the size of the camp I was taken to by the wing-man. And the place is crawling with his mutant friends. All sorts. Winged, gilled, furry, scaled . . .

I feel my top lip curl. They disgust me. All of them. Petra Crockett's right. They *should* be exterminated.

Using my boltdriver a second time, I remove the grille as quietly as I can and ease myself out of the opening. I look all around.

The floor is covered in a grey moss. Soft and spongy, it gives beneath my boots. All over the place are pieces of equipment from the Launch Times, zilched now and being used for other things. Upturned irrigation tanks serve as bedchambers, dining areas, nurseries. Turbine sails form walls to create separate living areas. Gantries have been turned to perches and roosting poles; convection pools, bathing areas . . .

I slide round the outer walls, keeping to the shadows, ducking down behind any item that offers cover. When I hear the sound of young voices, I shrink back behind a turbine sail. There's laughter and excited chatter. A couple of voices are singing. I peek out to see a group of children playing with scraps of discarded metal, which have been turned into makeshift toys.

Two of the children are bouncing up and down on springs that have been attached to their boots. Three or four are rolling steel rings with metal rods. And a little further off, a group of them are playing some kind of game with a huge polyprop ball.

It looks so ordinary. All right, so some of them have wings or scales, but they're just a bunch of kids playing, no different from the youngsters playing their simulation games in the Sanctuary.

When one of them falls over, grazes his knee and starts crying, the others gather round. And I stay where I am, crouched down and watching, as they put their arms around him, comfort him, ask him if he's all right.

And he sniffs bravely. 'I'm fine,' he says.

The ball game resumes, and I'm feeling confused. Back at the Sanctuary, it was all so clear cut. So simple. Humans good. Mutants bad.

But now I've seen these children I'm not so sure . . .

The next moment, though, I see something that dashes the doubt from my mind.

'Belle,' I breathe, spotting her over by a gantry.

Two mutants, one on each side, are holding her up. Her head's lolling. Her feet are dragging across the floor.

I ease my cutter from my belt.

The mutants lay her down on a metal trolley and trudge off. I check round. The place is crawling with mutants, and Belle's been dumped in some sort of holding area in the middle of them. It's not going to be easy to rescue her. But I've got to try. I put my hood up and cross the spongy floor.

I crouch over her. 'Belle?' I whisper. 'Belle? What have they done to you?'

'Who are you?'

I spin round, cutter in hand, to see the mutants have returned. They're holding whips and metal prods. They take a step toward us. One of them grabs Belle's arm.

'Leave her alone!' I roar, slashing at them with my cutter, sending them stumbling backwards.

A hand closes on my wrist. Belle's hand. It tightens painfully, forcing the cutter from my grip.

The mutants close in. They grab me and pull me away.

Belle simply watches.

They drag me over to a black pod, with power cables snaking over its smooth lid. It opens. They force me inside. It shuts. And the last thing I see is Belle's face, still staring back at me. I can't tell what she's thinking.

Then the white noise begins.

29

'York? Can you hear me, York?'

I must have passed out. It's Belle's voice. I open my
eyes and she's looking down at me.

The lid of the pod has been raised and Belle is
cradling my head in her arms. Her face is full of concern.
But I push her away, and she lets me.

I sit up. 'You're one of them,' I accuse her angrily.

'I don't understand, York,' she says.

'There's me, coming to rescue you,' I tell her, 'risking
everything. They shut me in that box – and you helped
them . . . Belle, I thought they were torturing you.'

'Torturing?' she says. Then her face breaks into
a smile. The smile I taught her. 'Something's gone
wrong with my battery-pack. They were helping me to
recharge,' she explains. 'When we were separated, I
followed you, York, to the outpost below the chimney.
But too late to stop the Sanctuary-dwellers taking you.'
She smiles again. 'I've been with my new friends ever
since.'

New friends.

I'm relieved she's all right, of course I am. But I feel betrayed.

'So now you're on their side,' I say bitterly.

'Belle is on no one's side,' a voice says. 'Except yours, York. I wish there were no sides. Now that you have been de-programmed, I'm hoping you'll be able to understand that too.'

'De-programmed?' I say.

Belle nods. 'The sleep-pods in the Sanctuary, York,' she tells me. 'They are fitted with a device to control thoughts and emotions. To suppress rebellion, to encourage loyalty. And every time you sleep in one, the effects get stronger.' She points to the pod I'm lying in. 'This has reversed that effect. Your thoughts are now your own once more.'

I swing my legs over the side of the pod and climb to my feet. We're in a dimly lit chamber, the ceiling and walls full of tech. Terminals, holo-screens, processors and data-stacks; lights twinkling in ever-changing constellations. A figure is standing by a screen, two feathered wings sprouting from her back obscuring my view of her.

Then she turns, and I see she is wearing a long flowing lab coat. Her yellow eyes fix on my face.

This bird-woman looks light and graceful, and I realize that the de-programming must have worked. The revulsion I was expecting is not there.

'Greetwell, York. I am Dextra,' she says. 'I am what the Sanctuary-dwellers call an Outsider. A mutant. We prefer to think of ourselves as Survivors.'

She pauses, head tilted to one side, watching my reaction to her words.

'Go on,' I tell her.

My body aches, I feel tired, but my thoughts are clear. I no longer feel the surges of negative emotion I experienced back in the Sanctuary.

'Doubtless the Sanctuary-dwellers have told you *their* version of the story. Now it is time for you to hear *ours*.'

Belle nods, and I sit back down on the pod.

'When the robots rebelled in the Outer Hull, and the bio-engineers sealed the Mid Deck to keep the zoids out, contact with the Inner Core was also lost. And almost immediately, without the central controls of the core, the containment and storage systems in the bio-zones began to break down. Specimens escaped, environments merged, laboratory seals were breached. And when *this* took place, the unity of the bio-engineers fell apart. One group wanted to retreat to an uncontaminated refuge. The others believed in staying at their posts, no matter what, in order to confront the growing chaos.'

She's talking quickly, her eyes intense and wings

trembling. I'm struggling to take it all in.

'Those who established the Sanctuary did so at a terrible cost,' she says. 'In order to build it, the Sanctuary bio-engineers seized the equipment and energy reserves that were meant to maintain the Mid Deck as a whole. They thought only of themselves – whatever their descendants might have told you.' She shakes her head, her expression one of sadness and anger. 'The Insiders,' she says. 'The three thousand.'

And I nod.

The Sanctuary had seemed so reasonable when Travis explained it. Now I'm beginning to understand that he only told me half the story.

'Because of the resources they stole, and still hoard in that Sanctuary of theirs,' Dextra goes on, 'the remaining bio-engineers – *our* ancestors – rapidly lost control of the bio-zones. We were made to retreat from forces we could no longer control and struggled to understand . . .'

'Accelerated evolution?' I say.

Dextra nods. Her yellow eyes blink.

'The Sanctuary would have you believe that accelerated evolution was an unfortunate accident,' she says, 'but the truth is that it was a key part of the science of the Biosphere.'

I shake my head. This is the exact opposite of what

I was told back at the Sanctuary.

'It was developed to make humans, and the world they brought with them from Earth, able to adapt to their new home. But after the robot rebellion, this accelerated evolution got out of control.' Dextra pauses. 'And yet it all could have been avoided,' she says, and I see her eyes cloud over. 'Droids maintained the seed banks and life labs of Zone 8 in complete safety, making sure the dangerous bio-research was securely maintained. But the Sanctuary re-programmed the droids to serve only its own needs, condemning the Mid Deck – and perhaps the entire Biosphere – to bio-chaos.'

I think of the critters in the Outer Deck – those strange life-forms that have adapted to the mechanical environment there – and recognize the truth in Dextra's words.

'But we, the Survivors, have never shared the Sanctuary's selfish vision. We have stayed here in the bio-zones and done what we had to do to survive and fight back.'

Dextra spreads her wings.

'Shortly after the robot rebellion, some of our ancestors took the brave decision to use this evolution technology to genetically modify their own bodies. They did this so they could continue their work in all parts of the Mid Deck, from the ice and cold of the polar zone

to the heat of the desert and the very depths of the ocean zone. With the droids gone, they had no other choice. It is a task that generations of Survivors have dedicated their lives to ever since, York – bringing the bio-zones back under control, containing and storing accelerated evolution in order that it can be used for its intended purpose.'

'To adapt life here in the Biosphere to the conditions they might face on a new Earth,' I say slowly.

Dextra nods. 'Unfortunately, only the Inner Core has destination data, so no one knew what to expect.' She sighs. 'Though none of that matters if the Mid Deck is lost.'

Dextra crosses to the bank of glowing lights.

'Despite what it looks like, York, we have made great progress. We have halted runaway evolution in all the specimens of the ocean, polar, forest and desert zones. And all this in spite of the repeated attacks of the Sanctuary.' Her eyes narrow. 'Yet, for all our efforts, Zone 8 has so far defeated us. Accelerated evolution there continues to run wild.'

I shudder as I remember the huge glowing creature in the sinister grasslands.

'And now, after five centuries, our energy reserves are almost exhausted,' she goes on. 'If Zone 8 is not tamed, then evolution will accelerate out from it once more – and this time, we'll have no way to halt it.'

Dextra turns back to me. Her eyes are bright and pleading.

'We need the Sanctuary's help. Their droids. Their energy reserves. The Sanctuary-dwellers themselves. By working together, we humans – humans of whatever form – can take back control before it's too late.'

I swallow hard. The detonation droids from the Sanctuary are on their way. I look back at Dextra.

'It might already be too late,' I say.

'They have discovered our main laboratory complex because of you?' says Dextra. Her voice sounds calm, but the feathered wings, still trembling at her shoulders, give her away.

'I'm sorry,' I tell her. 'When I retrieved the data-banks from that droid for the Sanctuary-dwellers, I had no idea of the real situation. I . . . I believed the lies they told me.'

She smiles sadly. 'It cannot be helped, York. We will try to save what we can.'

She looks at Belle, who nods at some unspoken understanding between them. Then she turns back to me.

'Go with Belle,' Dextra tells me. 'She knows what to do. If any of us survive the attack, we'll meet at the Citadel.'

And she turns and crosses the floor to a console set into the bank of lights over at the tech-station. I watch her for a moment as she hunches over the controls, her magnificent feathered wings forming an arch over her lowered head.

She is not
a mutant, I
realize. She
is just a human.
With wings.

A siren sounds, and
huge panels begin to open
in the roof like the petals of
some gigantic flower. Light from the arc-lights
floods down into the immense chamber.

This really is a hidden city, and it's incredible.

The Outsiders emerge from gantries, roosts, sunken

pools and adapted cabins, and fill the walkways and thoroughfares. They do not panic. Acting quickly and efficiently, they gather up essential equipment and data-stores and begin to make their way to evacuation points.

Heavy-set people with leather skin are climbing ladders up into the light, glowing power-nodes and heat-canisters strapped to their backs. Others, their bodies covered with thick fur, are gathering holo-units, info-pods and memory-stacks in clusters, and following them. I see gill-men and -women slip soundlessly into convection pools, carrying oval spheres fastened to urilium frames between them. They disappear into the depths.

Then suddenly the air is filled with the sound of beating wings, and I look up. The winged people have taken to the air. Some have feathered wings, some have scaly wings, and some, translucent golden wings, with skin stretched taut over a framework of slender bones. As they rise in the shaft of light from the open ceiling, I see that each of them is clutching a glistening cable. And as the cables go taut, the vital tech-units around me are lifted up into the air.

It has all taken moments, and yet it is an awe-inspiring sight – humans perfectly adapted to this environment . . .

'We must go, York,' Belle's voice breaks into my thoughts. 'This way.'

She takes me to the grille-covered opening to one of

the
ducts,
pulls the grille
off and tosses it
aside. Then she crawls
into the steam-filled interior.
I glance round and see Dextra.
She has not taken to the air
with the other winged Outsiders.
Instead, she is ushering a line of
children down through a hatch in the
moss-covered floor, her wings raised
protectively over their heads.

I swallow as a wave of guilt rises inside
me. This is all happening because of me.

All at once there is a deafening crash as the
floor of the chamber erupts, scattering turbine
sails, convection pods and insulation panels in all
directions. I see a black-helmeted head emerge,

followed by huge armoured shoulder panels and a metallic ribbed torso. Beneath are powerful propulsion units. The ribs of the torso are lighting up, one after the other, in a luminous detonation sequence.

Another head bursts up through the floor, and another . . .

Belle reaches out and hauls me into the duct, and we're running through clouds of hot steam when the blast wave knocks us off our feet. My ears are ringing, my lungs burn. I feel Belle pick me up, and we're moving again.

There's another blast, which I hear this time, a muffled *crump.*

Moments later, the blast wave propels Belle and me up out of the duct in a column of rushing steam. We land in a bank of sand outside and tumble, head over heels, to the foot of a dune.

I look up to see a dazzling flash of white, which is followed at once by an ear-splitting explosion. Shards of metal debris shoot up into the air in all directions as a great mushroom-shaped cloud of smoke rises over the hub-generator. Around us in the sand dunes, power lines snap and writhe, sending down a blizzard of sparks.

There's another explosion. Then another, and another, as Petra Crockett's detonation droids do what she sent them out to do: destroy the mutants' central lair.

A sandstorm breaks over us and I can't see. And with

the clamour in my head, I can barely hear either. It's disorientating. I feel Belle's hand wrap itself round mine, then hear her voice. It sounds like someone calling me from far away, muffled and hollow, the words coming and going.

'York . . . go . . . me . . . after the . . .'

I follow where Belle leads. As we get further away from the blast site, the storm of sand begins to thin. Suddenly she lets go of my hand.

There's a faint hissing sound as something flies past my face, blurred and indistinct. Then two more. And as the dust clears I see that Belle has three of the energy spiders attached to her. She falls to her knees and topples forward as they hungrily feed, draining her power supply.

I draw my cutter and slash at them, sending painful jolts through my arm as I make contact. I'm in luck. The insects don't resist. Releasing their grip on her, they scuttle away.

But Belle remains motionless, slumped forward on her hands and knees.

I reach towards her, only to freeze, stock-still. Above us, hovering over the lip of the sand dune, is a lens-head droid. There are two spindle-legs with it. One has a wing-man clamped in its pincers.

I hardly dare breathe. Perhaps the lens-head hasn't seen us . . .

I hear a *click* just behind me. But before I can turn my head, my world goes black.

31

When I come round I find myself upside down. The blood's gone to my head. I'm dizzy. I feel sick. I'm in the tight grip of a spindle-legged droid that is marching mechanically over the dusty ground.

I've no idea where I am.

Suddenly the jolting and jostling stops. I'm dropped. Land on the ground hard, awkward. My elbow jars. I roll over.

Belle and the wing-man flump down on the ground on either side of me. Belle is slumped over on her side, her face expressionless, her body stiff. The wing-man rocks backwards and forwards where he lands, his left wing bent back at an impossible angle. He looks across at me, squinting against the brightness of the arc-lights.

I recognize him. It's the winged Outsider who first rescued me from the golden-furred predators.

'You,' I say.

He nods, attempts to smile, then winces with pain.

We're in an enclosure. Above it, I can just see the visiglass at the top of a gleaming geodesic dome.

'The Sanctuary,' I mutter, half to myself, half to my companion.

The enclosure has a perimeter of metal walls, their surfaces splashed red like spattered blood. It's a pattern I've seen before – in the holo-simulation; the work of a clever vid-designer. Or so I thought.

But this is no simulation. It's horribly real.

All of a sudden, above the central wall, four huge holo-screens appear. In the outer two, I can see a sea of faces. They're from the dome. There's Lennox and Klute. And there's Travis. And there are thousands of others in rows behind them. Fact is, it looks like every single Sanctuary-dweller is there watching.

The two middle holo-screens are blank until, with a second flash and an amplified crackle, images appear on them. An empty podium with three consoles set on it in a line. And Petra Crockett's head.

It fills the screen, intimidatingly large. Her dark eyes focus on me.

The crowd stares attentively – at me, at her. The atmosphere's tense.

'York, York, York,' Petra Crockett says, her voice that silky soft purr. 'I can't pretend I'm not disappointed in you. We welcomed you into the Sanctuary. We gave you a home. And how have you repaid our friendship and generosity? With sabotage and treachery.'

Outrage rumbles through the crowd of Sanctuary-dwellers.

'You not only sabotaged our safe-suits,' she goes on, 'but you alerted the Outsiders to our plans.'

The rumbling grows louder.

'Your actions were reckless,' she adds, then frowns. 'Yet our plans were not thwarted.' She looks first one way, then the other, and she smiles, her lips parting to reveal the two rows of even white teeth. 'For I am pleased to announce that our detonation droids were successful.'

Now a cheer goes up from the spectators.

'They destroyed the Outsiders' lair.'

The cheering gets more animated. On the outer holo-screens, the Sanctuary-dwellers are clapping, slapping one another on the back and punching the air.

'And our surveillance droids have confirmed that there are no survivors. Every single mutant is dead.' Her voice drops. 'Except for one.'

A hush falls over the audience.

'This winged monstrosity,' says Petra Crockett, her voice cold and hard. 'Note its deformed breastbone. Note the inhuman curvature of its spine. The wings . . .'

A hissing and muttering comes from the crowd, which grows louder as their revulsion grows. Then the chanting starts.

'Destroy the mutant! Destroy the mutant! Destroy the mutant!'

Despite the pain he's in, the wing-man climbs stiffly to his feet. He raises his head and stands tall. I join him, and the pair of us stare back at the crowd defiantly.

Petra Crockett is unimpressed. 'The girl is York's companion,' she is saying. 'We've had them both under surveillance since they broke through the force-field from the Outer Hull. She willingly served the mutants from what we can tell. And she seems to have turned her companion against us.'

The crowd murmurs disbelief and horror. Someone boos.

'Which brings me back to our traitor, York, here,' she says.

The jeers and catcalls increase. And I notice that Travis has his hands cupped to his mouth and is booing along with the rest.

Petra Crockett fixes me with her steely gaze, and her eyes are so large on the screen it feels almost as though I'm being swallowed up inside them.

'There is a price to pay for turning against your fellow humans, is there not?'

Her head turns from side to side, as if in search of the answer from her audience. And they respond, screaming and shouting and waving their fists. She nods back at them.

'A price that will be extracted in full in the arena,' she adds. 'For our enjoyment. Who wants to play?'

'Me! Me! Me! Me!' countless voices shout out, and on the screen I can see the Sanctuary-dwellers jumping up and down excitedly, arms raised, trying desperately to get Petra Crockett's attention.

'How about you, Lennox?' Petra says. 'I've been following your progress keenly. Do you think you can entertain us?'

'I'd be honoured,' I hear Lennox say.

I watch him climb to his feet and make his way through the crowd to the podium. He looks unpleasantly eager, and I remember that he was one of the first to congratulate me – all smiles and kind words – when I arrived back with the droid's memory-unit.

'And how about you, Lisette?' says Petra Crockett. 'You show great promise at the simulation games.'

The crowd turns, and I find myself focusing in on a slim girl with dark wavy hair, who raises an open hand in triumphant acceptance of the offer.

'Thank you!' she cries, and beams as she strides to the podium. Again the crowd roars its approval.

'And . . . last but not least . . .' Petra Crockett says. She hesitates. The spectators fall still. Then a smile plucks at the corners of her mouth. 'Travis,' she purrs. 'Yes, you, Travis. Will you accept the challenge?'

He nods. 'I accept,' he says.

He picks his way through the crowd to join Lennox and Lisette. Unlike the other two, his face looks serious, but I cannot tell what he's thinking. He does not look at me as he takes his place on the podium.

The three of them pick up the consoles. Lennox is to the right, Travis to the left, Lisette between them. A grinning skull, its eye-sockets black, hovers on the screen beneath each of them.

The sinister, cheerful music begins to play as three lens-heads appear over the top of the metal enclosure and hover above us. Petra Crockett frowns, chops at the air with her hand, and the music falls silent.

'I think that on this occasion we should hear their cries for mercy,' she announces. 'And they should hear us,' she adds, looking around the ranks of spectators. 'So raise your voices, all of you. Let them know *exactly* how the Sanctuary feels.'

A cacophony of boos and whistles and howls of rage

echo round the arena. I know they're not to blame –
that the hours of darkness spent in the sleep-pods have
programmed their behaviour, like they did mine. But
that doesn't make it any less horrible. Or frightening.
Petra Crockett lets it continue for a while, then raises her
hands.

Once again, the crowd falls still.

Petra Crockett nods appreciatively, then she speaks,
the words calm and chilling.

'Let the game begin.'

32

Lennox and Lisette work their consoles with intense concentration. Their flying droids come at the wing-man from both sides, zapping him with their blue taser-light. Sparks fly and his body judders. Two tasers strike the back of his neck at the same time. He jerks violently backwards and slams to the ground with a strangled scream.

The crowd roars with excitement. The eye-sockets of two of the skulls light up a pale yellow.

Meanwhile, the third lens-head – Travis's one – drops down low and zaps Belle. Over and over, the taser hits her. Body. Shoulder. Neck. A glowing net-like pattern of lights covers her body as it convulses on the ground, but she makes no sound.

A chant goes up, 'York! York! York! York . . .'

Lennox and Lisette are enjoying torturing the wing-man too much, but Travis responds. His lens-head speeds towards me, its taser firing.

I dodge and dart as best I can. But I'm not quick enough. A bolt of taser-light hits me at the top of my spine. It's like being struck a hammerblow. My back arches, my eyes burn. I let out a cry of pain.

The crowd cheers.

A second blast hits me square in the chest. I'm thrown to the ground, body numb and head spinning. I look up groggily.

The eye-sockets of the third skull are now glowing the same pale yellow as the others.

I glance at Travis on the holo-screen. He could have finished me off if he'd wanted. I'm sure he could. But that's not the game.

And to think I believed this was just a simulation.

Looking round, I see that the other lens-heads are still

working together. Their anti-gravity tractor beams are on, and they're using them to raise the wing-man up in the air some ten metres above the ground.

'He's flying!' a voice jeers, and a section of the crowd explodes with taunting laughter.

The wing-man writhes and wriggles. His good wing flaps, but the other one is shattered and useless, and there's nothing he can do. He hovers there, unable to break free of the tractor beams – until they abruptly switch off, and the wing-man falls.

He lands hard in a crumpled heap and groans miserably where he lies.

The crowd roars with delight.

The lens-heads hover above the arena, and I brace myself for the inevitable pain. I roll over on the sand – and my gaze falls on Belle. She's stirring. Then her eyes snap open and she jumps to her feet.

The taser-light from Travis's droid has recharged her.

The spectators scream at the gamers, but before

Lennox,
Lisette or
Travis can
respond, Belle leaps
high in the air. She
seizes one of the droids
by the head and hurls it
at another as she lands. As
the two lens-heads collide,
they explode in a dazzling flash
of white and yellow. Zoid-juice and
molten metal shower down into the
arena.

There's a horrified gasp from the
crowd as Lisette's and Lennox's skulls turn
black on the screen, then disappear. No one
can believe what they're seeing.

Down on the ground, Belle shoots out
a leg with lightning speed, landing a
powerful blow on the remaining lens-
head droid. Its body panel crumples
and it crashes through the metal wall
before exploding.

Travis's skull turns black.

The groans of the crowd grow louder. Petra Crockett's jaw drops.

The three spindle-legged droids come towards us, their pincers outstretched, only for Belle to leap up onto first one, then the next, and rip off their head-units with her bare hands. She brings down the third with an enveloping tackle, crushing its knee joints. It crashes to the ground, fizzing and bleeping, before shutting down.

I spin round to look at the screens. The spectators are standing, open-mouthed. The three gamers are clutching their useless consoles, at a loss to know what to do next. Petra Crockett looks as though she's been sucking on something sour.

Then there's a fizz and a crackle. All four screens go blank.

Belle helps the wing-man to his feet. The three of us climb through the gaping hole in the metal wall.

'We've got to get to the Citadel,' Belle tells us.

'You know the emergency protocol?' the wing-man croaks.

He doesn't look well. There is a greyish tinge to his skin that matches the tattered flight-suit he's wearing, and his broken wing causes him to grimace with pain at every step.

Belle nods. She stoops down at the control panel of the first walkway we come to and re-activates it.

The walkway takes us swiftly away from the arena and the Sanctuary dome beyond. Already, Petra Crockett has sent lens-heads out to track us. But we've got a good head start, and when we hear the hum of their propulsion units, we jump from the walkway into undergrowth and watch them fly past.

We're on the edge of the rainforest in Zone 3.

The wing-man groans and sinks to the ground. His left wing is jutting out awkwardly, the broken bones clearly visible through the translucent yellow skin.

He looks up at Belle, then me. His sandy brown eyes crinkle up into a pained smile.

'My name is Cronos. Thank you,' he says. 'Thank you both.'

Then he closes his eyes, and I think he's passed out. But then, sighing and wincing, he sits up, and I watch as he reaches into the inside pocket of his flight-suit. He looks worried, checks the other side, and his expression relaxes.

He removes his hand, and I stare down at the thin flat pack in his grasp.

It's small, orange, and made of some kind of soft polysynth. It looks old. The colour's faded, the corners are worn. On the front panel, is a diamond-shaped silver shield, the words *Life Lab* and *Zone 8* embossed inside it.

Without looking up, the wing-man tears at the corner of the pack with his teeth. There's a soft hiss as the seal is broken, then he pulls it open with his fingers.

I exchange a glance with Belle. She's as intrigued as I am.

The wing-man extracts a square of paper-like material from the casing, so white it seems to be glowing, and so light that it floats in the air. Then he starts to unfold it. It doubles in size, then doubles again, and again and again, until it's the size of a sleep-sheet. It's transparent and tissue thin, and there's a faint smell to it too, I notice, a curious mixture of hot wires and wet soil.

The wing-man pulls the floating material over himself,

wrapping it around his body like a shawl. The material contracts, flowing across his shoulders and settling over the injured wing. Then it starts to glisten. At first, I think it's just a trick of the light, but the pin-prick flashes of silvery white increase and intensify, until the whole wing is glowing and giving off a gentle warmth that seems to pulsate rhythmically like a heartbeat.

Then, within this warm glow, I see that changes are starting to take place to the wing itself.

Slowly at first, but gathering speed, the jagged ends of the shattered bones come together. The splinters fuse. The fractures disappear. One by one, across the span of the wing, every broken bone is mended.

'That should do it,' the wing-man says at last, and smiles, and it is clear that the pain too has gone.

He straightens up and raises his wings. I see his breastbone brace and the knot of muscles at his shoulders flex. Then, tentatively at first, but with increasing confidence, he beats them back and forward, back and forward, till his feet leave the ground and he rises into the air in front of us. He hovers for a moment, then comes down to land and folds his wings behind him.

'We have three hours of arc-light left,' he tells us, and rolls his eyes. 'So long as they haven't been tampered with again.' He looks around him. 'It's not safe here. But I know a place.'

He turns and sets off through the rainforest on foot.
'Follow me,' he calls over his shoulder.

With Cronos leading the way, we stride out over the
spongy mattress of fallen leaves that cover the floor
of the rainforest. As we continue, I see how his eyes
dart from tree to tree, from plant to succulent plant. He
doesn't look happy. And he keeps muttering to himself –
about moisture levels, soil erosion, nutrient saturation . . .

All at once, he flaps his wings, and Belle and I watch
as he flies up to a cluster of gigantic cup-like blossoms
that sprout from the upper branches of a tree. He hovers
in front of them, examining the scorched petals closely,
before joining us on the ground and continuing on foot
without saying a word.

A little further on, he spots a clump of pink-topped
fungi. He crouches down to inspect them, and I hear him
tut. Then, plucking one of them, he slips it into the front
pocket of his flight-suit.

We come to a saturated area, where trees have
toppled from the grow-troughs and are lying criss-
cross on top of one another in thick oozing mud.
Remembering how I almost drowned in mud just like
this, I look at Cronos. He's shaking his head.

'More sabotage,' he says darkly, and spreads his
wings once more. 'Wait here,' he instructs Belle and me,
and takes to the air.

Just then, overhead, I hear the sound of hissing water, and I look up to see the dark shape of the giant rainmaker gliding through the air towards us. Its sensor-lights are flashing and the sprinkler nozzles are blasting pressurized jets of water down at the ground.

Cronos tilts his wings, first this way, then that, as he flies up through the branches of the trees and on beyond the forest canopy towards the arc-lights. I raise a hand to shield my eyes from the brightness, and watch as he swoops back down and lands lightly on top of the great irrigation unit.

He bends forward and opens a series of hatches along its side. He reaches in. Sparks fly, and his face is lit up in the glow. The sensor-lights dim for a moment, then grow bright again, and spread across the surface, until the whole rainmaker is a bright constellation of pulsing lights.

All at once, the sound of the hissing changes. It gets higher pitched and softer. The rushing becomes a gentle pattering, and as Belle and I watch from the cover of a tree, I can see that the nozzles of the rainmaker have untangled themselves and are fanning out, sending down a spray of tiny droplets that splash softly on the leaves of the trees below.

Satisfied, Cronos returns, his huge wings silhouetted against the arc-lights as he glides back down through the air. He lands beside us.

'The work of the droids,' he mutters grimly. 'The Sanctuary-dwellers use them against us, no matter what the cost to the bio-zones.' He shakes his head. 'To think of the good we could do, if only we all worked together.'

Cronos looks back up at the giant rainmaker as it continues on its way. And as it passes overhead, it showers us with a soft, refreshing rain.

I've got so many questions to ask him, but the wing-man clearly doesn't feel like saying any more. He strides off through the rainforest, looking around him, still muttering to himself.

Belle and I follow.

Then the arc-lights go out.

34

It's dark. The single arc-light still shining overhead barely penetrates the dense forest canopy.

Not that it makes much difference to us. Cronos knows the rainforest like the back of his hand. Trouble is, though, I'm feeling pretty tired. It's been a long, tough day. I'm wondering just how much further we're going to trudge through the dark rainforest when he suddenly stops in front of a tree and looks up.

'We can stop here for the night,' he says.

'Under this tree?' I ask, and Cronos smiles.

'Not down here, York,' he says, and points. 'Up there.'

It is the first time he's spoken directly to me – used my name. But then he's had a lot on his mind.

Belle crouches down. 'I do not need rest,' she says simply. 'I'll wait here and keep watch.'

Cronos looks puzzled.

'Belle's a zoid,' I tell him. 'We teamed up in the Outer Hull.' I glance at her and smile. Back at the Outsiders' central lair, I thought she'd betrayed me. I was wrong, of course, and I reach out and take her hand in mine, squeeze it. And she surprises me by squeezing back. 'We've been through a lot together,' I say.

Cronos's jaw drops. 'I overheard our bio-engineers talking about a robotic mutation they'd found in the zones,' he says. 'They were really excited about it.' He looks Belle up and down. 'So that was you. I had no idea. You look so . . . so *human*.' He turns to me and laughs. 'No wonder she dealt so effectively with those droids,' he says. 'Tech-engineering at its most advanced . . .'

'Belle's not a machine,' I break in. 'She's my friend.'

I notice that Belle is looking at us, back and forward, gauging our reactions.

'I see,' says Cronos.

'And York is my friend,' says Belle.

'As a bio-engineer myself, I find your ability to adapt to your surroundings fascinating,' he tells her, then looks at me. 'Belle might not need rest,' he says, 'but we bio-lifeforms certainly do. Allow me.'

Cronos takes me by the shoulders and beats his wings, and together we rise off the ground. Belle stays motionless below the tree, looking off through the darkness. Branches swish past, my feet catching on the leaves, and my stomach lurches as Cronos soars high above the forest. His wingtips are edged silver in the single arc-light. Then he dips down towards the treetops.

We land on a swaying branch, and I see it.

A tent-like structure, paper-thin but strong and well camouflaged, attached to the trunk of the tree. Cronos lifts the entrance flap to the little hideaway he's brought us to, and I crawl in.

It is spacious inside, with room to stand, and bedding in the form of rolled mats in one corner. In the other are bio-tech instruments and several of the globe-shaped white-noise weapons.

I roll out the mat that Cronos hands me. Made of the same sort of grey moss that carpeted the Outsiders' central laboratories, it's soft and warm, and as I lie down on it, I feel my whole body relax.

Cronos sits cross-legged on a mat on the other side

of the tree cabin. He takes stores from sealed canisters and prepares a meal – hydrating and steaming ration packs quickly, expertly. He hands me a heated tray of food. There's some sort of chopped plant, a mound of steamed grains and rich, textured protein. It smells and tastes delicious, and I don't need the Sanctuary's coloured pills to enjoy it.

'That medi-pack you used on your injured wing,' I say between mouthfuls. 'It said *Zone 8* on it . . .'

'You have a good eye for detail,' Cronos says, and smiles. 'Regeneration wrap, we call it. It can heal just about anything.' He frowns. 'You got anything you need healing, York?'

I check myself over. But despite the violence of the battle in the arena, I can't find a thing. Not so much as a scratch. I shake my head.

'Well, you let me know if you do,' he says, examining his own wing. 'Trouble is,' he goes on, 'regeneration wrap is ancient tech, produced back before the Launch Times, and there's barely any of it left now. And without fresh resources, we can't hope to research and develop any more.'

'So it's accelerated-evolution technology?' I ask. 'From the life labs of Zone 8?'

Cronos nods. 'It's one application. One of many,' he says and sighs. 'Accelerated evolution was perhaps the most startling discovery we humans have ever made. More important than learning to make fire. More important than managing to fuse the atom. It is the key to life itself. It enables us to alter the genetic code of every living organism. Plant. Animal . . .' He pauses. 'Human.'

He flexes the wings at his shoulder.

'Used properly,' he says, 'it could – it has – transformed mankind.' He shakes his head. 'Which makes it all the more tragic that such a discovery should have gone so terribly wrong . . .'

'Like in Zone 8,' I say quietly. The horror of the grass that seeded itself on everything, as well as the terrifying creatures that live in it, are still so clear in my mind.

'Like in Zone 8,' he repeats, his eyes glazing over for a moment as he stares into the middle distance. 'But all is not lost. Not yet,' he says. 'So long as there are a few of us Survivors left, there's still hope.'

Petra's words back in the arena echo inside my head. *Every single mutant is dead.* I only hope she was wrong.

Cronos dips his head, his wings folded at his back. For a moment, I think he's fallen asleep, but as I put down my empty tray, he speaks.

'I know we must look strange to you, York,' he says, and bats away my denials with a wave of his hand. 'But when the zones broke down, those who chose to battle on had to adapt themselves to continue the work.' He hesitates. 'But it is more than that, York . . .'

Cronos looks up at me. His expression is radiant, full of joy.

'Our ancestors chose their adaptations,' he tells me. 'Their gene-engineers spliced and grew the modifications they required. Since then, we have inherited their adapted genes and gone out into the Mid Deck to enjoy a freedom the Sanctuary-dwellers can only dream of.'

He's smiling. His eyes have a far-away look.

'To glide on the thermals through the arc-lights, York.

On your own wings! To roam the polar zone, impervious to cold. To dive to the depths of the ocean zone and swim with the whales . . .'

I lie down on my mat and listen as Cronos talks. His voice is deep and melodic, the grey moss warm and soft. Cronos tells me how he and the other modified Outsiders have built on the work of generations before them; have never given up hope, not only of surviving, but of creating a better world.

He reminds me of my friend Bronx, back in my home in the Outer Hull. Instead of biological modifications, Bronx used zoid parts that I scavenged to augment our bodies. My eyes close and I find myself drifting off to sleep. I think of Belle down there at the base of the tree, keeping watch.

Zoid. Wing-man. Me. We're really not so different.

The arc-lights come on full-blast. I sit up, feeling
completely rested; rub my eyes, look around. The tree
cabin's papery walls are glowing a rich golden yellow.

And I'm on my own.

I climb to my feet and step out onto the branch.
Cronos is up already. He's standing with Belle at the base
of the tree. The two of them look up when I emerge.

'Ah, York,' says Cronos. 'All set?'

Before I have a chance to answer, he spreads his
wings and flies up to meet me on the branch. Taking
my shoulders, he carries me down to the ground. Belle
greets me, and the three of us set off through the
rainforest towards the Citadel, where we are supposed
to meet up with Dextra. Given what Petra announced in
the arena, I'm beginning to wonder if there's any point.

Not that I'm about to give up now.

The rainmaker unit must have passed overhead once
more during the hours of darkness, and this time it's
done its job properly. The leaves are twinkling with
droplets of water and the air's humid. Neither Belle nor

Cronos seem affected, but I'm hot inside my flakcoat and activate the coolant device. Cold air flows, and as my body cools, I find myself missing the familiar feel of the skeeter's little warm body curled up at my chest.

Where are you, Caliph? I wonder.

We keep on through the forest, Cronos leading us now, Belle happy to follow.

The arc-lights start to cool. Beneath my feet, the leaves crackle and crunch, and I look down to see that they're edged with frost. The trees are bare and stick-like. I realize we must be approaching the polar zone.

'Is the Citadel here?' I ask Belle as we step into a freezing bank of fog.

'No, York,' she says. Then, her voice a whisper, she adds, 'Surveillance droids could be listening.' And she won't say any more.

I follow the two of them over the frozen ice crystals: the winged Outsider and the zoid girl. They both know so much more about this chaos zone than I do.

After another hour, despite turning the coolant device to heat mode, I'm painfully cold. There seems no let-up in the freezing fog. Then, just when I'm thinking we're lost, we come to the frost-covered wall of the ocean zone.

Belle turns to me. She's smiling.

'There,' she says, and I look up to see the frozen

waterfall towering before us. We stop at the bottom, where the crashing water has solidified into weird twists and huge boulders of ice.

Belle begins scaling the waterfall. She doesn't feel the intense cold and, with her hands and the soles of her boots able to grip effortlessly, she doesn't slip either. Me? I touch the surface of the ice, and it's so cold it burns.

Cronos taps me on the back. 'There's a much easier way up,' he says, gripping me by the shoulders once more.

On either side of me, I see his great wings lift up and begin to flap, and suddenly my feet leave the ground. As we fly up the frozen waterfall, the cold air it gives off chills my face, my hands, and my breath comes in puffs of white cloud. Cronos soars higher, and not for the first time, I marvel at his strength.

'The ocean breach occurred five hundred years ago, and the bio-engineers polar-coated the barrier to contain it,' Cronos tells me, pointing as we fly past. 'The breach was only the first of many disasters that occurred when the core systems were lost. Forest fires, floods, swamp slides and desert drift. And then . . .'

'Accelerated evolution?' I say.

Cronos doesn't answer me directly. 'As with the breach, we controlled all the other disasters,' he says. 'Except in Zone 8.'

We fly up over the frozen waterfall and, from this
height, I can really appreciate its scale. The jagged edges
of the ocean tank are crusted white around the column
of frozen water, sealing the hole. Above the breach, the
tank rises another thirty metres or so, and as we swoop
down, I see Belle powering her way up its frozen surface,
finding hand- and footholds in the ice.

Cronos and I land on a metal platform. It's fringed
with giant wave machines that jut out into the water. As
we wait for Belle, I cross to the edge of the platform and
gaze out at the vast ocean. It stretches off before me as
far as the eye can see.

There are ice-floes nearby, milky floating islands that
bump into one another as underwater currents drive
them on. There are creatures on some of them. White-
furred. Yellow-furred. Large and small. And others,
some with sleek grey skin, some with black-and-white
down, that slip off the ice and disappear beneath the
icy water.

In the middle distance, huge waves move across the surface of the ocean in parallel lines. Capped with white foam, they tip and fold over, and crash down on one another.

A black-backed bird with broad wings and a sabre-like beak glides over the rolling water, its head turning slowly from side to side as it scans below. Then, suddenly flapping backwards, it flips over and dives down, breaks the surface without a splash and disappears from view. Moments later it re-emerges, twenty metres or so further on, and flaps back into the air, a large silver fish hanging limply from its beak.

In the far distance, the colour of the water changes from dark green to an intense turquoise. Small submerged islands glow orange and pink and yellow. In places, they puncture the surface of the water, and are ringed with white as waves splash against them . . .

Hot swarf! The ocean zone is more wonderful than I could ever have imagined.

'Cronos! York!' Belle's voice breaks into my thoughts.

I turn to see that Belle has reached us on the platform. But she is not alone. Rising up and hovering out of reach above her is a lens-head.

Cronos reacts with great speed, pulling a globe weapon from his flight-suit and holding it up. It glows and emits a burst of white noise. The lens-head spins

out of control, and Belle
leaps up and lands a kick
that sends it crashing
to the platform. It
skids across the
metal surface
and comes to
rest at my feet.
Its lights flicker,
then go out.

Belle joins us as Cronos
and I are looking the zilched
droid over.

'We don't have much time,'
says Cronos. 'There'll be others
behind it.'

Just then, heads appear in the
water below the platform. Gill-people –
six of them – together with a transparent visiglass sphere
which bobs to the surface moments later.

Cronos picks up the droid and puts it under his arm.
'Follow me,' he says, climbing down from the platform.

The gill-people are holding the sphere steady in
the water as a panel slides back to reveal a circular
opening. Cronos climbs inside and settles himself in a
clear moulded seat. Belle follows him, and I take her

hand as I climb down after her.

Inside, we sit next to Cronos, our seats tilting back as we do so, and the sphere seals itself with a soft hiss. We start to descend, the water rising up around us higher and higher, until it closes over our heads.

The four gill-men and two gill-women go with us. At first, as they dive down into the water, plumes of silver bubbles shoot out from the sides of their necks, but they soon peter out as their gills take over from their lungs. With their hands at their sides, acting as rudders, their bodies ripple and their webbed feet flip up and down, powering them down through the water at incredible speed.

It looks exciting. These humans, modified with their wings, their gills . . . they're just so amazing.

An immense fish with fat lips and sleepy-looking eyes rises up from the depths. It swims beside us for a while, its mouth opening and closing as it feeds, before flicking its tail and swimming off, back into the shadows. A shoal of pale snake-like fish glide past, the tips of their tails flashing with an intermittent green light.

And then I hear it. Booming howls and lulling moans.

I recognize the sound straight away. I heard it before, in the chamber beneath the ocean. But now, in the ocean itself, it is twice as clear. I turn, and there, emerging from the shadows far ahead, is the great whale, its huge paddle-shaped flippers driving it through the water towards us. Its sleek body ripples with graceful movement; its tapered head tilts.

And it is not alone. There are three others with it; two as large as the first, the other a baby. They circle round us in great gliding spirals as we continue to move down, staring in at us with their dark, unblinking eyes. It's as if, like the gill-people swimming out in front, these huge ocean creatures are escorting us to our destination.

It is dark down here in the ocean depths, but suddenly the water lights up below us, and I realize that we're heading for a mass of glowing luminescence. As we approach, I see that it is made up of millions of

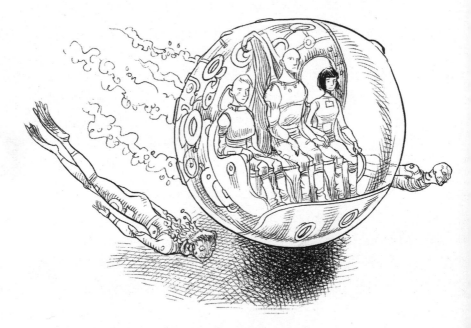

jellyfish with long dangling stingers and pulsating bodies. Immune to their poison, the gill-people swim ahead, and the jellyfish part as they get closer, creating a living tunnel for them to go down.

We follow the gill-people into it, and the globe is enveloped in blue pulsing light. At the centre of this living fortress is a visiglass sphere, a hundred times bigger than the one we're sitting in. We begin to slow, and up ahead I see figures, dim outlines, moving about in the interior of the larger sphere.

'Welcome to the Citadel,' says Cronos as we approach a circular airlock.

It opens, and we glide inside.

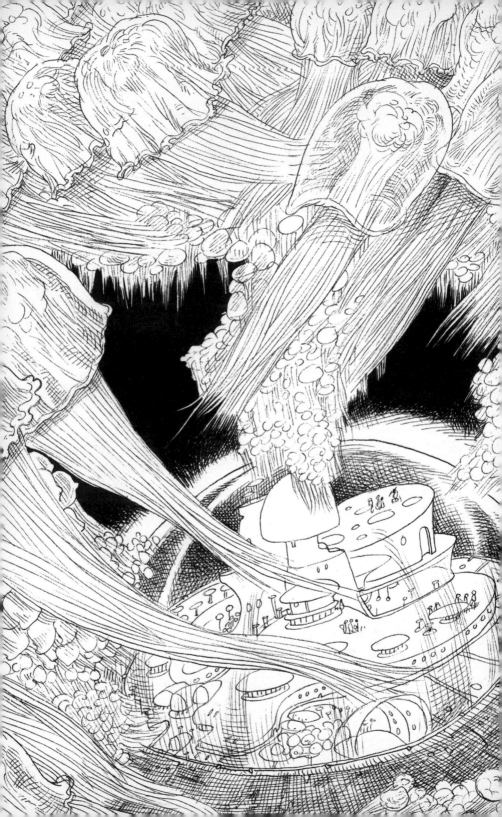

36

I stand looking out of the sphere of the underwater Citadel. Beyond its curved visiglass wall, the vast bloom of jellyfish swim in ever-changing patterns, providing the perfect camouflage.

Their translucent bodies flex and pulse, lacy frills ripple with glowing light, and long frond-like tentacles trail below them. Pink and pale yellow, lilac and green, the luminescence from the jellyfish lights up the sphere with a gentle shifting glow. I'm hypnotized by the strange, weightless movements of these creatures.

Of all the extraordinary zones I have come across in the Mid Deck, *this* is the most beautiful.

Cronos and the gill-people hurried off clutching the drone when we first arrived at the Citadel, leaving Belle and me by the airlock. I don't know how long we've been standing here, but I don't mind. I could look at the ever-changing display outside for hours.

Although the interior of the sphere is in semi-darkness, in the shimmering light I can see figures moving up and down the various levels. None of them pay us any attention. Finally, though, Cronos returns, and we follow him into the dimly lit interior.

Then I see Dextra. She's alive!

Standing on a raised platform in the centre of the sphere, Dextra is surrounded by data-banks and info-pods, holo-units and memory-stacks, and the oval spheres on their thin urilium frames – all the gear I saw the Outsiders rescuing from the hub-generator. It's up and running again now, screens flashing, circuits humming.

A fur-man is hunched over an info-stack close by. Next to him, a couple of gill-men are standing at one of the oval spheres, while just beyond them, a tall figure plucks and sweeps at the holo-screen in the air before him with scaly fingers.

Dextra, her wings outstretched, is quietly directing them all.

Cronos, Belle and I climb a flight of steps to join her. I look around me. There can't be more than twenty Outsiders here.

'Are these the only survivors?' I ask her, shocked.

Dextra lowers her wings and smiles. 'No, York,' she says, indicating the various holo-screens. 'We had prepared our evacuation procedures precisely. No one was lost.'

'Thank the Half-Lifes for that!' I exclaim. 'Petra

Crockett said you were all dead.'

Dextra nods. 'She would like it if that was true,' she says sadly. 'The Citadel is our info-hub of last resort,' she tells me. 'Unfortunately, it's not big enough to accommodate everyone. But from here, we can keep in touch with the others in their individual zones. And most importantly of all,' she adds, 'the Citadel protects our most precious resource.'

I look again at the rows of tech-gear. 'All this,' I say, nodding towards it.

Dextra laughs, a soft, gentle sound. 'No, York,' she says again, and passes a hand over a control panel.

At our feet, the surface of the platform becomes transparent, and I look through it to a lower level, where children are sleeping on mats of soft grey moss. Hundreds of them.

She passes her hand back over the panel, and the scene below vanishes.

'But their parents are risking everything out in the zones,' Dextra says, suddenly serious. 'Zone 8 is increasingly unstable. The entire bio-engineering hub has been compromised. Without more resources we will not be able to hold back accelerated evolution . . .'

Cronos nods. He, like Dextra, is looking at me intently. So is Belle.

'But before I ask you what I must ask you, York,' she

says, 'there is something I want you to have.'

She turns to one of the oval spheres on its urilium frame. It is packed full of kit – micro-data slides, weapon globes, containers of regeneration wrap . . . and my backcan. She picks it up and returns it to me. I haven't seen it since the raid on the Outsiders' camp.

'Cronos here saved it for you,' Dextra says. 'Open it, York.'

I take it in my hands. 'Thanks,' I say.

To be honest, the sleepcrib and ration packs it contains aren't that important. But I don't want to appear ungrateful. I hold the backcan up, and as I do so, I see movement through the perforations in the outer casing. I flick the switch at the top, the lid pops up – and a small furry head appears, nose twitching and eyes blinking into the light.

'Caliph!' I cry out as the little skeeter leaps up onto my shoulder, then jumps down into my arms. He's purring and squeaking, nuzzling against my chest, then lapping at my chin with his tongue. 'Caliph! Caliph!' I laugh. 'I thought I'd lost you for good!'

I look up to see Cronos and Dextra smiling back at me. Belle laughs, and I'm astonished because I'm not sure I've heard her laugh before.

'I told Dextra how much Caliph meant to you,' she says.

I stare at her, amazed. 'You did this for me?'

Belle nods. 'Because I like you, York. Because I knew it would make you happy.' She pauses. 'Because we are friends.'

And I don't know what to say. So I hug her. Caliph joins in, jumping from my shoulder to hers and back again; the three of us, reunited.

'Thank you. Thank you so much,' I say, stroking the little squirming critter; tickling his belly, his neck, behind his ears; pressing my face to his. 'Thank you all!'

When I look up again, the expression on Dextra's face has changed. The smile has gone, and her gaze is intense once more.

'There is something I must ask you to do,' she says. 'Something that will test your resolve to the limit.'

I look back at her. At Cronos. At Caliph . . . and Belle.

'Name it,' I say.

37

I walk towards the great visiglass dome of the Sanctuary. The lens-head droid hovers at my shoulder.

I'm terrified. But there's no turning back now.

As I climb the stone steps, the circular door of the airlock slides open, and inside there are two spindle-leg droids waiting to meet me. I take a deep breath and go in. The lens-head follows. The airlock shuts behind us, and I'm back in the decontamination chamber.

A panel in the ceiling opens and the lens-head rises up and disappears through it for its own decontamination protocol.

'Decontamination sequence activated,' comes a familiar voice.

The visiglass tube descends. The red lasers cut away my clothes and turn them to ashes. My skin is probed and prodded. Antiseptic spray wafts over me, then the jets of warm air.

I'm given the all-clear, and dress in the Sanctuary clothes laid out.

The lens-head reappears at my side as the protocol

ends and the door ahead of us hisses open. I walk through into the atrium – and am confronted by Travis.

He has a pulser aimed at my head. Behind him, Sanctuary-dwellers crowd the cavernous hall, while others stare down from every level of the dome, their faces pressed to the visiglass.

'On your knees, traitor,' says Travis.

I do as he says.

Petra Crockett is speeding down towards us in an elevator. All eyes turn as she steps out and strides across the floor towards us. As she approaches, I see that her face is drained of all colour; her lips pinched and thin.

She clearly wasn't expecting to see me again.

'Please, Petra,' I begin. My mouth is dry and my voice cracks. 'You must give me a chance to explain.'

Petra stops beside Travis and glares down at me.

'Explanations are unnecessary,' she says, and her voice is cold and hard. 'We all saw what you did in the arena . . .'

'*I* didn't destroy the droids. Belle did!' I protest. 'She's a zoid, manufactured in the Outer Hull. She turned against me, when all I wanted was to get her back from the mutants.'

Petra stares back at me, the expression on her face a mixture of disbelief and contempt.

'And I'm sorry I sabotaged the safe-suits,' I go on. 'But I heard Travis pleading with you to mount a rescue mission, and I didn't want any of you to risk your lives. For me, the safety of the Sanctuary and everyone who lives in it comes first, and always will.'

I'm talking quickly, looking first at Petra, then at Travis, then at the other Sanctuary-dwellers. I spread my arms. There are tears in my eyes.

'Forgive me, I beg you,' I plead. 'I've learned my lesson. Belle was a machine, nothing more. But you . . . you are my friends.'

Petra Crockett still looks sceptical.

'Belle was programmed by my people back in the Outer Hull to serve. To serve *me*. But then, when we got separated, the mutants tampered with her motherboard. They made her serve them instead.' I shake my head. 'I was such a fool to have tried to rescue her. You see, I overheard you ordering the destruction of the Outsiders' lair, and I went there for my zoid. It was a mistake.'

Petra Crockett raises an eyebrow.

'But I swear to you,' I say, meeting her gaze, 'everything I did was with the best of intentions. When I reached the mutants' lair, Belle betrayed me to them. I was their prisoner. There was nothing I could do. I'm only thankful that the detonation droids arrived when they did. The mutants were totally wiped out – but Belle was *still* going to kill me. If your droids hadn't found us when they did, I would be dead.'

I feel hot, sweaty. I'm speaking faster and faster, my voice trembling with passion.

'And later, in the arena,' I go on, 'I didn't have a chance to explain. You were all there – my fellow humans, my *friends* – looking down at me and I so wanted to tell you everything. To explain. But the pain . . .'

I leave the word hanging in the air.

I survey my audience. People are nudging one another, whispering behind their hands. Travis, too, looks uncertain. He has lowered his pulser.

'And yet you went with them,' Petra Crockett says,

her icy voice cutting through the atmosphere. 'The winged mutant and the zoid girl. The last transmission from the surveillance droid here showed the three of you standing on a platform in the ocean zone.'

She folds her arms.

'I was their prisoner, Petra,' I tell her again. 'The winged mutant used his globe weapon to disable the droid. But I have scavenged it and brought the evidence back here to the Sanctuary. So you can see for yourself what actually happened.'

For a moment, Petra Crockett says nothing. She's frowning, her eyes thoughtful. Then she gives a little nod to Travis.

'My chamber, now,' she says. 'Bring York and the droid.'

The elevator whisks us to the upper chamber; me, Travis, the lens-head droid and Petra Crockett herself. After the hubbub and tension of the entrance hall, Petra Crockett's chamber is a haven of peace and tranquillity.

Holo-screens flicker into life around the chair at eye level. Conversations, hundreds of them, murmur from panels in the synth-moulded head-rest. Info-cables which sprout from the arm-pads pulse with data.

The chair is supported by a single arched urilium stem, which revolves slowly as Petra surveys the images in front of her. There are views from all over the Sanctuary. The bev-counter, the crèche, the gym, the sleep-pods . . . Plus more images from outside, which are being sent back by lens-heads in the zones.

From her vantage point in this chair, Petra Crockett seems to see and hear everything.

The lens-head droid I brought with me hovers beside the chair and connects itself to one of the info-cables. I can see the dent from Belle's boot on its black body.

Petra waves a hand and twenty-eight holo-screens

become one. It's dark at first. Then a bright scrawl of lines appear – which abruptly settle down to a clear picture.

And there's the ocean-zone platform at the top of the frozen waterfall.

Cronos is standing to one side of me. He's got a globe weapon in his hand. Belle's next to him, her head half turned away as she scans the vast green and turquoise ocean.

'There's no one here,' she's saying. 'Just like in every other zone. They're all dead.'

Cronos waves his weapon at me. 'Thanks to him,' he snarls.

Belle turns. Her face looks impassive. 'What shall we do with him?' she says.

'Kill him,' Cronos tells her, and smiles unpleasantly. 'Slowly.'

Belle nods grimly.

She takes a step towards me, one hand outstretched, and is about to seize my arm when I twist sharply round and seize the weapon from the wing-man's grasp. Belle lunges towards me. But I'm too quick for her. I activate the globe, and a blast of white noise makes the image pixillate and break up.

When it reappears, Belle is lying on the platform. She shakes and judders as a blue light spreads out all over

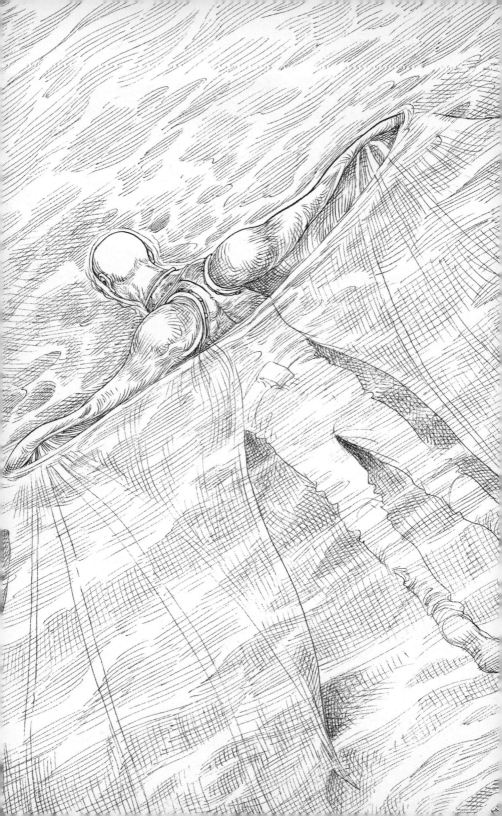

her body. Her hair's on end. Her eyes roll back till only the whites are showing. Her head snaps forward in one last spasm of movement . . .

Then nothing.

In front of me, Cronos slumps to his knees, his wings crumpling behind him. There is a cutter embedded in his chest. My cutter. His blood-covered hands clutch hopelessly at the handle.

I see Petra Crockett wince, but she doesn't look away.

Up on the holo-screen, I lift a boot and push the mutant firmly in the back. He topples from the platform and, arms and legs flailing wildly, hits the water. Cronos sinks, then comes bobbing up to the surface. And there he remains, wings rigid and outstretched, floating face down in the water.

Then the image jumps and my face appears, large and close up. I'm staring directly into the lens, my eyes blazing with a mixture of anger and delight.

'Death to all mutants!' I roar.

Then the screen goes black.

'The mutant's weapon damaged the transmitter node,' I say. 'But fortunately, not the memory banks.'

Petra Crockett nods. She swivels the chair round and eyes me levelly. My heart's thumping in my chest. Has she believed what she's just seen? Has the fake vid-clip convinced her?

She smiles. 'It seems I misjudged you after all,' she says quietly. 'You did well, York.' She turns to Travis. 'Make sure that everyone understands York's change of status.'

'I will, Petra,' says Travis. He takes me by the arm. 'Now how about a celebratory drink at the bev-counter?'

The two of us turn and head back towards the elevator.

'Oh, and Travis,' Petra calls after us. 'You can cancel that order for a new birth.'

39

The celebrations continue late into the night. The arc-lights go out, the dome lights come on, and still the bev-counter is buzzing. Everyone has seen the surveillance droid's transmission and wants to know what it felt like killing the very last mutant.

They talk excitedly of plans to sterilize the zones outside the Sanctuary, unopposed by the Outsiders. Controlled detonations. Forest incinerations. Vacuum-draining the ocean zone and ejecting the water vapour through vent ducts up into the Outer Hull. I sip my satzcoa, nod and smile, as the Sanctuary-dwellers describe an idealized Mid Deck, scrubbed clean of all contamination.

Nobody mentions Zone 8.

'Come on, then,' says Travis at last. 'Let's get you back to your sleep-quarters. You're one of the three thousand now. And after a good night's sleep, it'll be as though you never left.'

I wait for a little while after he's gone. Around me, the lights dim and the Sanctuary-dwellers close the lids

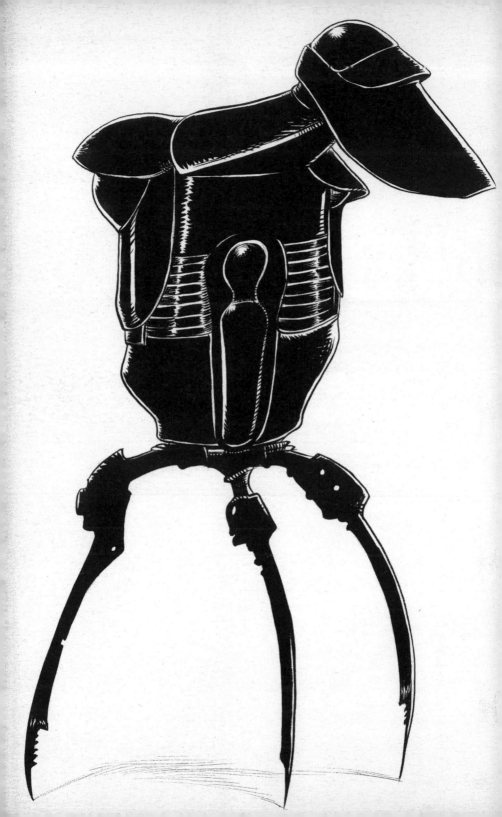

of their sleep-pods. Up near the top of the dome, Petra Crockett swivels in her chair.

I take an elevator.

'Level one, twelve, twenty-four, twenty-six,' I say, relieved that I can still remember the number.

We come to the armoury. I step out, cross the floor and enter the room next to it.

The droid store.

It's eerie inside. Droids, hundreds of them, lined up in rows, fill the cavernous space. Lens-heads, spindle-legs, new shiny-black detonation droids. I shudder as I see their black-helmeted heads, armoured shoulder panels, ribbed torsos . . .

It's such a waste, I realize. Dextra was right. The rich resources of the Sanctuary stored here should be used for conservation, not sabotage and destruction.

I walk past row after row of lens-heads. Some look new. Others are waiting for maintenance repairs to be done before they're sent out again into the zones.

I recognize my droid at once from the deep, triangular dent that Belle's kick left in the middle of its tubular body. I slide my hand round to the back of its head and flick a switch. The visiglass lens pops up and, fingers shaking, I remove a small, glowing data-chip.

Tiny, insignificant. Overlooked.

I slip it into the pocket of my crisp, white Sanctuary

tunic, then take the elevator up to Petra Crockett's chamber. As I step inside, I hear her voice from the far end of the chamber.

'Can't sleep, York?'

I look round, and glimpse her through a half-open

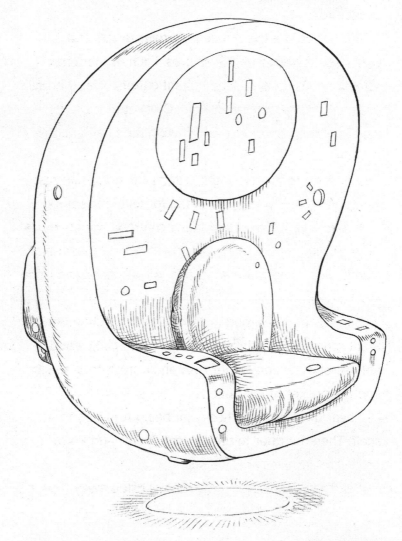

door. I hadn't noticed it before. It leads into some kind of cabinet, concealed and private. Of all the people in the Sanctuary, Petra Crockett is the only one who has a place to hide away.

'I'll be right with you,' she says, and the door is pushed to.

But not before I've noticed the rows of jars and wire baskets stored on the shelves. Each of them has something inside it. Pickled mutant critters. Weird body parts . . . I remember what Petra Crockett once told me about the importance of knowing the enemy, and I shudder.

'I'm sorry to disturb you so late,' I call out. 'But I just wanted to thank you again, Petra, for taking me back.'

I edge towards the chair in the centre of the chamber.

'York. York. York.' Petra Crockett's voice is soft and lilting. 'Please, no more apologies. All you need is a good night's sleep.'

There is no sleep-pod in Petra Crockett's chamber that I can see. Only this chair with its info-cables and holo-screens. I run a finger over an armrest, then reach into the pocket of my tunic . . .

I hear the clunk of a heavy jar being returned to a shelf. Then the door to the cabinet opens, and Petra emerges. Her eyes are shining.

'My chair,' she says, and smiles as I step away from it.

I smile back. My tunic pocket is empty. The glowing data-chip is pulsing in the cable hub on the underside of the smooth, sleek armrest.

'I have perfected it over the years,' she says. 'So that I can watch over you all, protect the Sanctuary at all times.'

She sweeps past me and sits down. The chair swivels as Petra leans back in it.

'Every system, every droid and sleep-pod, every elevator and airlock . . . *everything* runs through here. And I see and hear it all.' Her eyes narrow. 'You were in the droid store.'

I nod. 'You were right,' I tell her. 'I couldn't sleep. Too much on my mind. The droids down there, they make me feel safe. I know this sounds foolish, Petra, but I was thanking the surveillance droid that saved my life. If it hadn't recorded what really happened back in the ocean zone . . .'

'So that's what you were doing!' Petra Crockett gives a soft laugh, and her smile broadens. 'Get to bed, York,' she purrs, that voice of hers so silky smooth. 'And sweet dreams.'

I open my eyes. The sleep-pod opens and I climb out.

Everything has changed.

The Sanctuary is alive with activity. Every elevator is crowded, speeding one after the other, down towards the atrium entrance hall. All three thousand Sanctuary-dwellers are spilling out across the floor, flocking to the outer visiglass panels and staring outside.

Or rather, two thousand, nine hundred and ninety-eight of them, to be precise. Only me and Petra Crockett are not caught up in the excitement.

I see her looking down at me. She knows something isn't right in this perfect little world of hers. She climbs into an elevator. I wait as it comes to a stop on my level. The door swishes open. I step inside and join her.

'What's going on, York?' she demands furiously. 'What have you *done*?'

The door closes and we descend to the entrance hall.

'Come and see,' I tell her.

Petra Crockett strides out into the crowd of Sanctuary-dwellers, but no one seems to notice her. They

251

are all too intent on staring through the wall of visiglass at the scene outside the dome.

Standing in a vast crowd are the Outsiders. They have come from all the zones of the Mid Deck. Gill-people; fur-people; scale-people; winged men, women and children. They are staring back at the Sanctuary-dwellers.

None of them move. None of them speak.

Then one of the Outsiders steps forward. A tall man with feathered wings. He has a youngster in his arms, a girl, her own wings folded back on her shoulders. They stop beside the visiglass wall and look inside.

The Sanctuary-dwellers watch them.

Slowly, deliberately, the wing-man raises a hand and presses his palm flat against the visiglass. He smiles. The girl in his arms waves uncertainly.

I hold my breath.

At first, nothing happens. But then one of the Sanctuary-dwellers steps forward. He looks like Klute, but older. He raises his own hand and presses it to the hand of the wing-man, fingers splayed, and only the pane of visiglass between them.

'Greetwell,' he says.

Suddenly a cry goes up. Everyone's moving at once. Sanctuary-dwellers and Outsiders, they're coming together. Mothers and fathers, small children and babes in arms. Curious at first. Then happy to greet one another, the sound of joyful voices filling the air.

The sleep-pods have done their work.

The Sanctuary-dwellers have been de-programmed and told the truth. Their minds are free, their thoughts are clear.

All of them are human. All of them are one.

Petra Crockett stamps her foot. 'Enough!' she cries. 'They are mutants, and mutants must be destroyed!'

But nobody is listening.

'I don't want to live like this,' a young woman cries,
and pounds a fist against the visiglass wall,
'imprisoned in this sterile bubble.'

'Let us out!' someone else shouts, and a
murmur of agreement ripples through the crowd.

'Droids! Droids!' Petra Crockett is shrieking.
'Destroy the mutants!'

'I've de-activated your command protocols,'
I tell her as I walk across to the entrance.

'The sleep-pods. The droids.' I smile. 'The
airlocks . . .'

I turn and place a hand on the
sensor-pad. The airlock doors
open. All of them.

'No! No! The contamination!'

Petra Crockett screeches. She turns and flees back to the elevator.

Dextra and the Outsiders walk through the open doors and pour into the dome. And the Sanctuary-dwellers surge forward to meet them. There's laughter. And there are tears. Children are hugged and Sanctuary-dweller and Outsider alike comfort and congratulate each other.

Belle, Dextra and Cronos come through the swirling crowd towards me, and the four of us embrace. Travis joins us. He is wide-eyed and ecstatic.

'I woke up this morning, York, and I knew all this had to end,' he tells me. 'I had such dreams . . .' He looks at Dextra, then at Cronos. 'I dreamed I had a brother. He was just like me, but with wings. We flew together, over the forests and grasslands, skimming the ocean waves. And I was overwhelmed by this feeling of oneness, of freedom . . .' Travis frowns. 'Of purpose.'

Dextra nods. 'There is so much that we can achieve,' she says, 'so long as we work together.'

Travis pulls back. He nods towards the top of the dome.

'Petra,' he says.

41

When we reach her chamber, Petra Crockett is sitting slumped in her chair. Above her, the holo-screens are showing images of the celebrations we left behind.

Winged figures are swooping past the visiglass walls, with waving Sanctuary-dwellers held in their arms. Others – both Outsiders and Insiders – mingle on the stone steps and set off along the moving walkways in clusters. People point and marvel at the zones around them.

Droids are assembling. Lens-heads hover beside spindle-legs awaiting orders.

Petra Crockett looks up at Dextra, Belle and me.

'I have lost control,' she says desperately. 'You!' She glares at me. 'You have overridden my systems.'

'I have,' I say simply. The data-chip that I smuggled into the Sanctuary has worked perfectly.

Petra's top lip curls with disgust as she looks at Dextra.

'You have destroyed my Sanctuary,' she says, her voice rasping now. 'Everything I've worked for.'

'It's not too late, Petra,' says Dextra, taking a step towards her. 'Don't you see? If we work together, we can bring accelerated evolution back under control. And with the resources of the Sanctuary, we can repair the zones and restore the Mid Deck. For everyone.'

Dextra reaches out a hand and takes one of Petra's. Petra Crockett flinches at her touch. Her face drains of all colour and her expression twists into a grimace of disgust as she tears her hand away.

'You . . .' she whispers. 'You . . . have . . . contaminated me . . .'

I see her hand reach out. A trembling finger hovers over a black sensor-pad, then presses firmly down.

There is a *click*.

'Termination sequence activated,' says a voice.

A circular visiglass screen rises up from the base of the chair and seals Petra inside it. She stares back at us, before a burst of red laser light blots out her horrified face. When it fades, the screen lowers to reveal a pile of ash.

'Termination sequence complete.'

Dextra turns to me. There are tears in her eyes. 'She must have been an incredible bio-engineer,' she tells me, her voice catching in her throat. 'To maintain all this. She could have done so much to help us. Instead, she kept us apart.' She wipes away a tear. 'But now she is gone.'

I feel a hand on my shoulder and look round. It's Belle.

'You did well, York,' she says. 'But there is more to be done on our mission. We must continue.'

42

The place is dark. Banks of data-drives, info-decks and tech-stacks surround us, and the air is filled with a low humming sound. We are in an underground life lab, deep at the heart of Zone 8.

Outside, the droid army has stopped the spread of accelerated evolution, and the grassland has been contained. Finally the chaos zone is being tended the way it always should have been.

'We will never manage to recreate the well-ordered bio-zones of the Launch Times,' Dextra explains. 'Not without access to the control systems of the Inner Core. But the evolved life can be managed and conserved.'

The Inner Core.

Our next destination. Now that the Mid Deck is functioning once more, it is time for me and Belle to continue our journey to the next level of the Biosphere.

'Are you sure about this, York?' Dextra asks – not for the first time.

She is standing beside me, Caliph crouched down on her shoulder between her wings, chittering uncertainly.

It's as though he knows that something's going to change.

'I'm sure,' I tell her. 'I'm glad we could help you here in the Mid Deck, Dextra. But there is still a war raging in the Outer Hull between humans and zoids. The answer to the robot rebellion lies at the Core,' I tell her. 'And I made a promise to my people that I wouldn't stop till I found it.'

'Even if that means leaving all this behind?' she says.

I look back at her. At Caliph.

I nod.

Dextra reaches out and takes hold of my hand. She squeezes it warmly.

'And this is the only way?' she says, and I hear the concern in her voice.

'The breach in the Inner Core has made it too dangerous a place for humans to go,' says Belle.

She is lying in the black pod next to mine. The two of us have already discussed what we have to do.

'No one could survive the radiation,' Belle goes on. 'But we are all data. A series of digital impulses. Our consciousness will travel to the Inner Core, but our bodies will remain here. We shall return to them when we have completed our task. If we can,' she adds.

'We'll keep them safe for you,' says Dextra.

She's smiling, but her eyes look moist. She closes the lid of Belle's pod, then mine, and my world goes black.

Whatever awaits us at the Inner Core, there is no going back now.

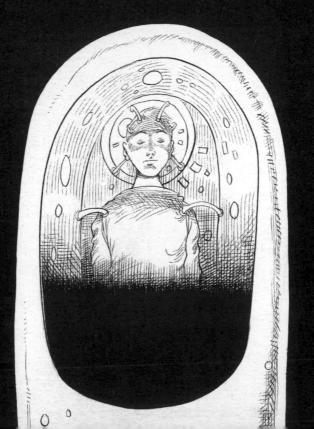

Look out for the next book in the thrilling

SCAVENGER

series . . .

Coming soon!